Co

Contents

This New North

edited by

SJ BRADLEY &
ANNA CHILVERS

Valley Press

First published in 2021 by Valley Press
Woodend, The Crescent, Scarborough, YO11 2PW
www.valleypressuk.com

ISBN 978-1-912436-57-6
Cat. no. VP0178

Cover and text design by Peter Barnfather.

Editor's Note

SJ Bradley

This New North is an anthology of new voices from the North. During my time as director of the Northern Short Story Festival, we were approached by the Walter Swan Trust who were eager to support programmes that developed new writing and new voices. We ran an open submissions process, aimed at writers who were already writing short fiction, taking it seriously, and who had already had some pieces published. We were hoping to find six new authors to take through a structured critique and mentoring programme, aimed at developing their voices.

We knew there was a lot of talent in the North, but perhaps what none of us had realised was exactly how much talent there was. The programme drew a lot of interest, and we received over sixty eligible submissions. Regretfully, we had to turn down a number of very good entries, and it was testament to the broad range of talent that we took the decision to expand the programme and run two critique groups, totalling twelve writers. As I write this footnote, the programme is now being run for a third time. I don't doubt that there will be more than enough talent to fill it.

The initial twelve academicians that went through the programme were: Haleemah Alaydi; Jenny Booth; Sarah Brook; Eva Bohme; Jean Davison; Melody Clarke; Trina Garnett; Jenna Isherwood; Andrea Hardaker; Lizzie Hudson; Dan Robinson; and William Thirsk-Gaskill. Most of the stories here are new, except for 'Umeboshi' by Eva Bohme, and 'Artefacts' by Jenna Isherwood, which first appeared in *Disclaimer* magazine.

Three additional stories that appear in this book are by supporters of the programme. Anna Chilvers mentored both groups of writers. Barney Walsh offered support to the programme by providing critique and enthusiasm, and Richard Smyth offered targeted critique and mentoring. Richard Smyth was also the Northern Short Story Festival writer in residence in Middleton Park, South Leeds. His story, 'Everywhere's in the Middle of Everywhere', was commissioned as a part of that residency. Special thanks to Friends of Middleton Park and the park ranger, Graeme Hall, for their support of the writer in residence programme there.

Foreword

Anna Chilvers

When the Northern Short Story Festival asked me to run workshops with their academy students, I was delighted. What a great job! Teaching creative writing is always exciting; it is a privilege to watch people take their first forays onto the page and begin to develop their own voice. But this was taking it a step further. We knew these guys were all great writers – they'd had to apply and were chosen partly on the strength of their work. The point was to help them to develop further, to move on, to push their writing to the next level.

From my point of view it was easy money – they submitted the work, they discussed it with each other – all I had to do was be there and listen. It was hugely enjoyable to spend time with people who were so committed, so generous, so eager to explore the boundaries of storytelling. The academicians all knew the basics of a story, they weren't there to learn that. The discussions revolved around how far the form could be bent, stretched and subverted. The writing was exciting and brave. The sessions were a safe place for testing out what worked, and getting feedback from other writers who were properly engaged with what you were doing. There was an atmosphere of playfulness, a freedom to try out new and innovative ideas.

The short story is a really exciting form, in that it allows for experimentation. If you were writing a novel and you chose to write in the second person, or from the point of view of a cheese-grater, or as though you were viewing all the incidents in the story from the top of a tree – you could of course, but you'd risk losing your readers. A cheese grater can only take you so far before you decide it's just too hard to engage with. The writing may begin to grate on your nerves by chapter six (see what I did there!). But a short story is by nature short – generally no longer than one chapter of a novel – and your reader is much more likely to accept the strangeness – to revel in the weird and unexpected.

This collection gives us plenty of that. The stories will unsettle you and delight you. Some of them were work-shopped in the Academy sessions, and some are new stories written since. They show the breadth of styles and approaches to storytelling, and give some idea of the scope of what the short story can do. I hope you enjoy reading them as much as I have.

A Very Private Confession

Haleemah Alaydi

It was late April when I started eavesdropping on the
Hadads' conversations. All I said was, 'It won't happen
again'. But it did; sometimes intentionally and other times
accidentally when I went to the basement room to get
something out of the freezer for lunch.

This was the problem with some things; once you start
doing them, it is not easy to find your way out. Like
smoking, for example. Gabriel, my half Moroccan, half
Spanish boyfriend, tried to convince me to quit. I liked
him so much, so I only ever did it when he was outside
the house. Now I do it all the time, especially when argu-
ments get particularly heated between the Hadads, my new
neighbours. We had never been properly introduced, except
for the time I went over to their house to deliver a parcel
which the postman had left with me when they were out.
Rayyan opened the door, took it and thanked me. Later
that night when I'd arrived back from my evening exercise,
after running around the block thirteen times, I heard
Celmira and Rayyan talk about how sweet I was.

What I found strange was that I could hear the Hadads
from every room in our house. But it was in a small room
in the basement where I discovered that I could clearly hear
the Hadads' conversations. I struggled to hear things at
times, but I could make out the sound of the TV, the bang
of doors, the buzz of telephone, the flush of toilet, the
random chants from the other side, the lovemaking.

I was gradually introduced into the Hadads' lives. Celmira and Rayyan weren't happily married, although I've heard them share moments of intimacy and passion every now and then. Celmira had finished her doctorate in Education from the University of Oxford, and Rayyan was a banker, I guessed. I heard him once talk to Celmira about opening a Lifetime ISA.

'It'll help us buy our first house. Not only that, but we can also use it to fund our retirement when we both reach sixty. Awesome news, isn't it? There's also a bonus of up to £1,000. We could travel the world, buy new furniture … we could do anything we want.'

'Sometimes you forget that you're talking to your wife, Rayyan. I'm not one of your customers,' Celmira responded.

'What do you want me to talk about then? The weather?'

'I don't care if you talk about the weather, the sky, or the fucking Maldives, Rayyan. All that you talk about is money and saving and banking. It's just money, okay? I just want to talk about normal things like other people.'

'But darling, we need to think of the future. Our future together. I can't live in the city anymore. I want to move to the countryside. I'm sick of cities and cramped houses. I feel like I'm going to have a heart attack and die. I hate these hundreds and thousands of Leeds identical brick houses, identical kitchens, identical toilets, and I hate the parks, the corner shops, the pedestrian crossings, the university students jogging at 9 am. I hate them all,' Rayyan said.

'Why are you making a fuss about it? Seriously, it's a bit too much,' Celmira said. Rayyan didn't strike me as the type of person to take scenic strolls or live in the countryside. I saw him in Asda down the road stocking up on frozen pizza, and when I caught sight of him I turned and pretended to be distracted by the discounted African pineapples. I swept off before he could see me. My footsteps clacked down the road.

'I know it's a difficult conversation. But let's talk after you've had your tea. Okay?'

I heard them kiss that night. At the beginning, I struggled to hear things clearly, but I learned over time that I could hear better if I stepped a little bit further from the wall or if I held a glass against it, allowing sound waves to travel from one side to the other. It helped that Gabriel was working all day outside the house, in his studio. Our life wasn't interesting. I liked having the Hadads in my life, especially when I struggled to find auditions and casting calls in the North. Gabriel was a painter. And when he wasn't painting, he was chasing after buyers and art enthusiasts at fairs and conventions to sell his artwork.

'Did you get in touch with your imagination?' Gabriel asked. We once heard about this technique in a documentary show about the art of acting. I pretended to not know what he meant, so he elaborated more. I thought it made him feel good.

'I guess I'll have to try harder next time.'

'Take it slowly. Don't rush into it. Rejection is part of the business.'

'But I can't be bad at every audition I go to. Am I that bad? Tell me! Be honest.'

'It's not as simple as that. So, you go for an audition. There's only one part, and one hundred actors come to audition for that part. Fifty of them were good. Can they hire all Fifty? Absolutely not. They pick the actor who is best suited to the role.'

'I never get chosen for any part!'

'Did you work on your body language?'

I liked Gabriel. He was sweet. I don't remember a time when he made me feel bad about myself. Even if I was bad at acting, he'd always tell me to give it a go. Sometimes, he'd act as an expert on a subject he didn't know anything about.

I'd been promising myself not to eavesdrop on Celmira and Rayyan's private conversations. Unless I thought something unusual was happening. Like that time when Rayyan tried to burn Celmira's arm with a lighted candle after discovering she had been emptying every bottle of alcohol down the sink. She claimed that he was an alcoholic and had addiction problems, and he admitted that she disgusted him all the time. Rayyan called the emergency services. By the time an ambulance finally carried her in, Celmira had gone into shock. I watched from my bedroom window as they came back hours later without saying a word to each other. Later that evening, I spent a long time trying, without success, to press my ear against the wall, watch from the window, and follow the sound waves from the basement to hear their conversations. Suddenly I saw, in my mind, that I was acting in a feature film, playing a single mother, and Gabriel was impressed with my performance. I understood that it was terrible to think about this while Celmira was in pain. But that understanding didn't mean I could change how I felt.

Gabriel and I never argued. Maybe because we shared a lot of interests, such as a passion for arts and music. On Friday afternoons, we tripped into a shared obsession with cooking. We read hundreds of pages' worth of cookbooks, trying the recipes on friends and family, hunting for new flavours together. But things had changed between me and Gabriel over time; he started to eat out and come home late every day. I was okay with how things were in our life, until Gabriel started spending his weekends at his parents' house.

Even when he did spend the weekend at home, all that he wanted to do was to watch operas followed by documentaries on the performances he had seen. He'd rave for hours about the singers' technical proficiency, tonal quality and ability to sing dramatically and interpret the words so that their fortissimo sounds overjoyed, angry, scared or painful. Luciano Pavarotti, Giuseppe di Stefano and Maria Callas were some of his favourites. Then there was physical acting. He'd talk about their ability to sing while moving, crouching or lying on stage compared to those who only sang in a straight, standing position.

One thing I didn't understand was how Gabriel could've attended so many classical music concerts and still treat opera as if it were some particularly great art form. As if listening to someone screaming in a foreign language without even making out the notes and the words were things that differentiated musically literate people from others who had no appreciation for great music.

I made all sorts of excuses to listen to Celmira and Rayyan's conversations. At times, I'd told Gabriel that I needed to shower or prepare for tomorrow's audition or turn the stove off. Once, walking down to the basement, I heard Rayyan and Celmira joking about sports commentators. I must have had missed the context of the conversation. I didn't see what was so funny about sports commentators. It made me angry when they made references and jokes and told stories in bits and pieces that never came together because they'd break out in laughter. They never bothered to explain what any of it was about, as if I was never there.

Some days, I'd spend hours in the basement room listening to Celmira and Rayyan talk about their plans for their first child. Later that year, in September, Celmira told Rayyan that he was going to be a daddy. I heard him cry that night. I couldn't help but cry a little too. I wondered what they would name their baby. By the time I came to bed that night, Gabriel had already fallen asleep. After a year or so had passed since we met, Gabriel and I were no longer so unaccustomed to our love, and the fervour of our romance gradually disappeared.

For weeks, Gabriel and I didn't touch or kiss. After a while, I struggled to even recall the last time that I'd seen Gabriel naked. And after we both turned twenty-nine, I worked out that it had been seven months since we last made love. I thought that the reason might be because he was struggling to find inspiration for his paintings. Sometimes, he sat in his studio for hours doing nothing. When I tried to offer help, he said he didn't want to talk about it, because he didn't want to become self-conscious about not being able to find ideas. He said that he created these little crises as a kind of a secret strategy to push himself. I told him that he shouldn't wait around for an idea to occur to him. Gabriel didn't paint for weeks. I was worried about him, so I called Serena, his friend and painting colleague. She said that he was working on something major and asked, 'Did he not tell you?' and I answered no. She asked if Gabriel had stopped surprising me, or if we had lost interest in one another, to which I answered, 'I don't know.'

At first it was just the scent, and then it was other things. I didn't want to wallow in thoughts about what went on between Gabriel and Serena, so I was glad when Gabriel came home and checked on me the following week. For a moment, I considered confronting him. 'But,' I thought to myself, 'no. He didn't do anything to be ashamed of, did he?' So we spoke. First about the weather. Then Gabriel said he was doing 'just fine.' Had found inspiration for his painting. Was taking Spanish classes at the language centre.

For a while, I covered our bedroom walls with inspirational posters. I wrote a list of all his half-finished pieces and rough sketches. We watched interviews of his favourite painters in order to look out for anything to motivate him to paint. I hated having to pretend that it was unfortunate that Gabriel struggled to find inspiration for his paintings. I wanted to let him know that things weren't going well in my acting career, that things weren't going well in our life.

What he truly didn't know was how lucky he was. In fact, there was a part of me that believed that Gabriel knew exactly how lucky he was, but that he also knew that, as an artist, there were all these strings he could pull to induce sympathy, love, and compassion, to buy excuses, to make mistakes, to fail, to explain himself; and that he intended to pull those strings until they broke.

I'd asked myself what I could have done to make him more comfortable, feel more important, more loved, more anything. Was he not satisfied? Was he not happy? I could have cooked for him, I'd thought. The women at the supermarket had spoken about 'the way to a man's heart is through his stomach.' Oh, there was always more one could do to keep someone happy. I should have made him Bolognese, creamy with a rich tomato sauce, I thought, and I should have attended more opera performances with him.

I thought about Rayyan and Celmira that night. Had Celmira truly believed that Rayyan was the right one for her? Had she never wondered why he was taking a yoga class at 9 pm on a Sunday? Had they stopped being so unaccustomed to their love?

I assumed that everything would be fine between Gabriel

and me. And that was why I'd planned not to tell Gabriel about the new part I got in an upcoming feature film. I didn't want him to feel that he was behind on his projects and discourage his progress.

One night in early autumn, Gabriel finally decided to show me what he had been working on. He took me to his studio, and before revealing the painting, he came closer and kissed my cheek. I stretched out a trembling hand and stroked his neck gently, feeling as though it were a stranger's body I was touching. How could one look at the face of the only person they love and still feel so misunderstood, so unfamiliar?

When I saw the painting, I sank to the ground, too shocked to register what to do next. I could not bear to look into Gabriel's face. The painting was of a woman who was pressing her right ear against a bedroom wall. On the other side of the wall, there was a couple making love. Each stroke had a smudging quality that rendered the image watery. Every colour was bold and painted with such precise lines that it almost looked like a mosaic. Perhaps this was how Gabriel had seen me; empty, without anything of substance inside. Perhaps I was the stupid one, the good one, the one who gave too much, the one who cared too much. I hoped there was more meaning in my bones than tumbling colours, chaotic and shallow. But I was there leaning against the wall, lonely and unloved. Only when Gabriel continued to tell me that a seasoned Swedish collector had offered to buy the piece for $10,000 did I felt sick to my stomach. It took a moment for the words to sink in – or maybe the idea that he discarded my feelings as nothing important. Gabriel also told me that for the sake of harmony he had found an apartment, but didn't really go into details. I forced myself to speak, but nothing came out. For a moment, I could do things like this, stop answering, stop talking, and it was fine.

The next morning, I saw Rayyan and Celmira carry some packed bags and boxes down into the garage and pack their car. Celmira stopped to look at the house, tears welling up in her eyes. Not knowing if they could see me, and not even trying to hide myself, I wanted to run out to them, grab them by the shoulders, squeeze them and beg them to stay. But by the time I had zipped up my jacket, they had already gone. When I got downstairs, I saw that I had received a letter from Gabriel in the mail. My name was written at the top in Gabriel's awkward, childish handwriting.

I peered cautiously out of the front door and saw their car in the distance. I could feel the roots of loneliness creep through me when they drove off. I wondered if they had moved to the countryside as Rayyan had wanted or if they had gone somewhere else. I felt betrayed and also that I had betrayed others with my silence and my actions, and I didn't know how to make those I love the most stay.

It wasn't until I came downstairs three days later that I noticed the letter from Gabriel that I had forgotten to open laid flat on the kitchen table. There were no signs of remorse, or frustration, nothing revised or rewritten. On the contrary, the lines were pristine and even. Nothing was scribbled out. The paper hadn't been crumpled up or even folded. I reached out to open it, because I thought that was what I was supposed to do. But I didn't. Instead, I imagined that I was with the Hadads, driving away from town.

In September, it started to rain. Like clockwork, for four hours each afternoon. A young couple came past, walking their small dog, and I smiled at them. They were my new neighbours. I wondered if it would be awkward to say hello. Should I let them know my name, that I live right across the street, in the house with the red door?

Part of me longed to see the Hadads. Will they have sex on the day of moving in? Who will climax first? Will Rayyan drop onto Celmira's body? I wondered briefly whether their marriage would fall apart or if they would live happily ever after. It had stopped raining that night. The street looked beautiful, glowing neon in the downtown lights. Yes, it was cold. But it was the sort of cold that gave me a feeling of elation followed by deep sadness, made me want to break into a run. It was the sort of cold that made me have a sudden urge to go into clothing shops, buy knitted jumpers and allow myself to look different.

Boy's Own

Jenny Booth

He sits at his desk and the tone of the school bell fades into the slow chant of Latin verbs. It seems as though he knows the words without thinking. At first he chants with the others without listening until gradually he forgets to speak, mouthing the words as the sound becomes a background noise of the world like the sunlight that comes in through the window, warm on the wood of the floor, softening the polish on the desks. He lets his gaze wander over them all, the backs of blazers, the straight scissor cut censuring the hair from the nape of the neck and the collar. The boys in front of him scratch their heads, yawn, look round in turn. He looks out over the playing fields, a border of elm trees switching their leaves green/grey in Morse signals of infinite complexity. The rugby posts stand still and white like a memorial to their Saturday matches, steaming breath on frozen mornings, blue gooseflesh woken to pain by the slam of a tackle, a trickle of blood made sluggish by the cold brushed away in a smear of mud. A memorial to the two sides moving up and down the pitch, first giving way, then on the attack, while their peers stand at the side in dark coats and cheers echo off the old walls of the library and the empty quadrangle up to the skylarks.

In History they study The War. Blue and white photos show square jawed men holding bayonets and loading shells like heroes in films. He almost believes he has heard the air raid sirens and hidden in the shelters, that he was actually there, a white-faced child in a wool coat and cricket cap holding onto his Mickey Mouse gas mask, dark eyes lit up by the flashbulb in the Underground during an air raid, surviving for Britain. At home there's a photo of his grandad as a young man smoking a pipe in front of an artillery gun, his hair parted, smiling for the camera. After History they swap stories; France, North Africa, Burma; infantry, Special Forces, RAF. Stephen tells the story of his grandfather. Over the shipyards of Hamburg, his squadron turning their wings for home with the dawn behind them, a burst from an AA gun shot him out of the sky. Everyone is silent. The boy imagines life opening and closing like the shutter that preserved his grandad as a young man settling questions of honour and self-sacrifice beyond doubt. He says, 'That is the best story of all,' and no one disagrees.

Stephen is the boy's best friend. Stephen's hair is dark and curly and the boy's is fair. He is a centimetre taller than Stephen. Stephen is better at Latin. But otherwise they are the same, inseparable. The white marble memorial on the chapel wall for former pupils who died in The War reads: 'Greater love hath no man than this, that a man lay down his life for his friends.'

This is how a man loves his country, how a man loves his friends. This is how he loves Stephen and how Stephen loves him.

In Mathematics the master, his back turned away, demonstrates trajectory on the blackboard. Stephen mirrors him to the silent glee of the class, calculates angle of elevation, initial velocity, drag, imagines the parabola perfectly so that the ink pellet from his ruler rises, falls, hits the bare neck of Radcliffe in the front row on the sweet spot below the hair line. The bloom of ink expands on impact, and Radcliffe turns round and exclaims with alarm. The class erupts with appreciation. What japes! The master, more concerned with dispensing justice swiftly than fairly, singles the boy out for laughing the loudest and canes him in front of the class. He takes it silently, without a word of denial or excuse. He sits down and doesn't look at Stephen, refusing to take the look of gratitude he knows is being offered to him. After all, Stephen would do the same for him.

There is an unwritten code. Don't lie. Don't snivel. Take it like a man. Don't snitch. Stand up to a bully. Stick up for the weaker man. As a nation we love the plucky underdog. We were the plucky underdog, alone in Europe facing down the bully Hitler. From a pill box in the Kent dunes, he scans the horizon of the too narrow English Channel for the silhouettes of German destroyers. In that strange summer of 1941, the city emptied of women and children, the weather too gloriously hot for hiding, he stands at the wicket and looks up at the sky. They hear the motor of a V2 rocket cut out overhead, and hope where it lands won't blow the bloody bails off.

The boy is in East Wing coming from the refectory, engaged in animated negotiations with Stephen over a trade of comics for marbles and a Latin crib sheet. Around a corner Oliver Ingles, a disagreeable fellow in the Upper Fourth, holds Colin Mouldsworth, the First Form scholarship boy pinned against the wall by his collar. The boy doesn't hesitate. Stephen is his second, holds his blazer for him. Oliver is the bigger man but out of shape. The boy concentrates on footwork, keeping his guard up skilfully against Oliver's powerful but clumsy strikes and then, when the bully is out of puff, dispatches him howling down the corridor with a well-aimed straight left to the nose.

In the city the boy walks in the shade of libraries and bookshops with ink prints of cathedrals on the walls and philosophy texts with gold letters and maroon covers. He walks under arches with Latin words written above like magic spells, over stone lintels into the university courtyards of flowering chestnuts. The breeze is blowing the river into ripples. Willow fingers dangle in it. Someone's hat flies into the water. Inside the cathedral the low breath of the organ bounces up the pillars to the splayed fingers of stone holding the arched roof. Light comes in through the tall angular windows and lies on the floor in coloured squares. Long dusty banners hang above the altar. Flowers perspire on the font. Knights lie in repose on stone tombs in stone armour. Saints nailed to crosses of different designs bleed out of the glass, while sorrowful women in brown robes kneel at their feet.

On Sunday they walk up the hill to chapel. During the service the headmaster reads from the Bible. His voice rolls through the nave and past the choir stalls, whispers round the tops of the organ pipes, makes the bronze vibrate gently in the belfry. The candles flare smoky and orange as they stand to sing with a muffle of cloth and paper. From the congregation the voices of women raise uncertainly, wavering around the true notes, but he barely hears them. He stands next to Stephen and their voices rise over the fug of the flowers on the altar, the cross, the pigeons on the lightning conductor, to a point somewhere above in the blue.

After the service old ladies come up to the boy and warble their praise for the singing, touch his hair. Their skin is fragile and decaying like flower petals held for too long. They stand on the lawn, the men in dark suits, the women's dresses dazzling on the green, oriental flowers, birds of paradise. He wears a suit underneath his surplice. A suit is like a uniform. The school is like a university. The chapel is like a cathedral. A fight is like a war. When he grows up, he will be like his father. He will study at the university. He imagines himself standing in the cathedral gardens after a shower of rain, thinking thoughts like the white roses that wind in and out of the cloister windows while birds shake raindrops off the leaves. He will marry and have children of his own. He will love a woman like the words on the white marble plaque on the chapel wall.

Walking with Stephen just past the infirmary in North Tower, they turn a corner when who should they find but Oliver Ingles, an ill-favoured rough fellow from new money somewhere in the North. He has cornered Ruth Draper, the scholarship girl from Dyer House. The boy hesitates to wonder, when did they start letting girls into the school? But then he gathers his resolve, hands his jacket to Stephen and squares up to the bully. Oliver is the bigger man but poor fitness lets him down. After a few wild swings Oliver tires quickly and a well-placed right hook to the nose stops him in his tracks. When his fist makes contact with Oliver's face the boy is shocked. It feels real, like it could be him being hit. Blood starts running out of Oliver's nose. Ruth looks at him strangely, as if she is scared of him too, even though he isn't the bully.

In the freezing morning the boy crouches in the mud, his eyes fixed on the white goalposts. He catches the ball and runs with it, gritting his teeth as the crunching tackle hits. It isn't pain that he feels, so much as a terrible shock that carries him away from the pitch, away from all of them, to a redness behind his eyes. When he can see again, they are bending down to him. He remembers not to cry. He manages to stand up.

'It's only a scratch,' he says with a careless laugh. Blood is coming from his head. The game has stopped. They carry him to the infirmary. His mother comes to visit him. He is embarrassed by her crying.

'I'm fine,' he says and brushes her hand away.

They sit singly at their wooden desks in naval uniforms and Eton collars in Singapore, Calcutta, Port of Spain, Nairobi, Penang, Rangoon. The turning earth glides through ovals of shadow and still somewhere the sun rises on a boy in a pressed white shirt standing to demonstrate a trigonometry problem or the position of ports on a chalk coastline. The boy sits obediently facing towards a point unknown, the wool of his blazer a ward against the decaying tropical air. Outside a brown man hoses the playing fields to make them green. Beyond their boundaries the temples' intricate carvings corrode. Birds and monkeys scream from the trees above the vendors in the dusty streets and rickshaw drivers quarrelling over fares. He studies diligently, wins prizes in Latin and Mathematics and as a reward is transported away, a slim figure waving one arm uncertainly from the deck of an ocean liner. He embarks, his grave face dark under his straw boater, dazzled on lawns, an anomalous negative framed in the gothic archways at Cambridge. He will return to his country, to captain it like he captained the House Eleven or, rejecting this, to conjure up a new djinn out of the temples and bazaars, a floating apparition to battle the other, made up of everything that the other is not, Godzilla and Mothra slugging it out above the cities.

The master demonstrates history on the board, crossed cutlasses at Plassey, Amoy, Rorke's Drift, but the boy can't concentrate. His gaze drifts to Stephen who trawls blotting paper across his inkwell to the silent glee of the class. It rises, falls, hits the bare neck of Williams, sitting in the front. The ink stains his white shirt, Williams puts up his hand, appeals. The class erupts and the boy joins in as loud as anyone, waiting to be called to stand in Stephen's place. But the master, who doesn't like a snitch, a sniveller, who is more concerned with dispensing justice swiftly than fairly, says to the boy in front, 'A little ink isn't going to make you any blacker now, is it?' and the laughter grows.

Rows of terraced houses rise on the hill in tiers like a photo of the first XV or a tea plantation. Train sidings run along the backs of houses past lines of washing hung out over allotted squares of lawn. Children in uniforms duck into a shop for sweets, lunchtime chips, cycle with no hands on the handlebars, ride the bus kneeling up on the seats to stare out at the factories and the gasworks. School is like a job. One uniform is like another. But once a year the bus driver cuts his engine, waits two minutes to take his fare, the cyclist brakes and bows his head and women with shopping stop, caught in the magic spell. The silent bank of televisions in the shop window zoom in on the napes of the necks of the men in suits as they kneel in front of the white marble to place the red wreaths.

At the weekend the boy goes to the city and reads the Latin words over the entrances to the university, the cathedral, the courts. He reads them out loud, then realises he has never been taught any Latin.

As a nation we love the plucky underdog. We were the plucky underdog. In Amritsar, he didn't hesitate, raised his rifle. With a hand as steady as his resolve, his eye as clear as his conscience, he fired. They couldn't take it like men. The coolies in Singapore and Burma he had licked for insubordination and laziness squealed like cats. He rousted the

29

natives in Kenya out of their forest. They weren't so brave by the light of day and he made them jump for it in the camps, by George. Outside the bungalows at Cawnpore he wiped the impertinent sneers off those dark faces that had terrorised the Memsahibs. There were more of them, but they had no conditioning, no backbone. A few sharp rounds quickly dispatched them howling, while unarmed bodies lay silent in the dust, red stains blooming on white cloth.

After lunch they watch something about the war on television. But he doesn't understand. There are no blue and white men loading shells with open smiles. There are just women, screaming, pulling at their hair, crying, demanding, as if something unfair had happened to them.

In class, something has happened. Ink spatters the walls, on the far side of the classroom Wilford protests about his stained shirt. The teacher walks over to the boy and pulls him out in front of the whole class who watch, rapt with appreciation.

'Was it you?' the master demands, doesn't wait for an answer. Stephen is pretending to look out of the window. The boy thinks, take it like a man. Don't snitch. Don't snivel. But when the cane hits him, he is surprised to find how much it hurts him. It scares him. He thinks he is going to cry. He says weakly, 'But it was Stephen who did it,' and everyone laughs.

When he puts up his hands to try and defend himself the next stroke breaks his finger.

The early sun behind the elms casts long shadows on the pitch. Their breath hangs in the air. The two lines move backwards and forwards between the goals. The ball comes in an elegant parabola and the boy catches it, running swiftly forward. He passes one of the opposition, then another, swerving smoothly. He evades their tackles easily. It's almost as if they are letting him. The whistle blows and he stops, holding the ball, confused. Someone comes over and snatches the ball angrily. Play resumes. He joins in again, moving into space, but no one passes him the ball.

'Wait, whose team am I on?' he asks, trying to clear up the mistake.

Somewhere between the Third Form common room and lower school dormitories he is cornered by Oliver Ingles of the lower Sixth, fly half in the school team and captain of the debating society. The boy squares up to the bully bravely, remembers his footwork, keeps his guard up. But Oliver's punches seem to smash straight through. His own fist is slammed back into his nose. He partially stops a heavy blow to his cheekbone which swells and throbs. His whole body shakes and he feels very tired as if the adrenaline has worn off, but Oliver keeps coming. He remembers how he looked up to Oliver, listened to his voice carry the choir in church, watched him lead the first team through scrums. Stephen, his best friend, turns the corner then, sees and stops. The boy can't help but cry, snivel, reach out to Stephen. There is blood dripping from his nose. But Stephen looks round, embarrassed, brushes him off, says, 'Leave me alone will you, you're always following me round, staring at me.' Stephen walks away quickly.

In the shop window, the bank of televisions blink together like one giant eye. Horse chestnut lint drifts in the summer air as men with rolled up shirts pore over maps, census data, drawing people and nations into existence with good Indian ink and a solid grounding in the Peloponnesian Wars. At Hola Camp they break for tea. The boy tries to be calm, to understand why he is crying, why it hurts, but the words for this seem to float just beyond his reach. He sees himself, bloody, broken, weeping on the floor. He tries once again to speak, but the only words that come out are, 'I don't know who he is.'

Ark

Sarah Brooks

We move into Grandmother's body slowly.

It begins with my brother and his computers. The rest of us don't share his passion – the house being very small, and very full of the five of us – but if we try to object he tells us at length that computers are a vital part of our print culture that must be salvaged at all costs. They proliferate.

He asks Grandmother to look after his collection, because she never refuses him anything. She worries he'll turn into one of those boys who likes sport and beer and loud displays of male dominance, and she's so relieved when he shows no interest in any of this that she indulges him however she can.

'Just pop them in here, pet,' she says, gesturing to the little back room she sleeps in. Before long there's no space on her shelves or table or dresser, and only a narrow path left on the carpet from the door to her bed.

'Don't they creep you out a bit?' I ask her, when we're both perched on her bed with cups of tea, surrounded by the blank faces of the machines. 'They look sort of … expectant.'

'Don't be daft,' says Grandmother.

It's only when my brother keeps bringing home new computers that we realise Grandmother is swallowing them.

'It just seems a convenient solution to me,' she says, her hands folded on her stomach.

When Mum shouts at my brother for being selfish, he decides he'll move into Grandmother too.

Of course, with all the computers, and then my brother

as well, Grandmother has to do some growing. She lies on her bed, with a knitted blanket over her, and grows. When her foot bursts through my bedroom wall, Dad says we have to do something. 'It's just not decent,' he says, and makes us sew together all our bedsheets in order to have something big enough to cover her. The thin walls of our house are no match for Grandmother's body. She pushes through them like rice paper. We've moved anything valuable by the time she brings the floor down, the bricks and dust settling around her, and Mum's carefully tended garden swallowed up by debris. At that point, it just seems simpler for the rest of us to move in as well.

In fact, living inside Grandmother has some distinct advantages. Firstly, it's always warm, with plenty of soft, cosy corners for us all to retreat to, thus avoiding the need for long, awkward social occasions. Secondly, we find that Grandmother provides fertile ground for the sowing of crops. We grow strong and plump, our hair glossy and our skin bright.

My brother hooks the computers up to Grandmother's nerves. Grandmother learns quickly. Soon her words spill out in small, careful letters on the screen. She tells us what's going on in the outside world. Her friends bring her pillows and giant blankets to keep her warm. They're all envious, she says, and are trying to encourage their own families to move into them. 'Though they should have thought about this earlier, when they were bragging about all their grandchildren at university.'

We keep her alive as long as possible. We plant her favourite food and hack into the local TV station to get her favourite soap operas. We sit up late into the night telling her stories.

'She'd never just abandon us,' says my brother, but in the end she does.

We feel her go. We feel the walls of her body loosen and sag, feel the air still. Silence falls. Walking is hard, without the rhythmic pulse of her heart to quicken our steps. The first thing my brother does is turn to the nearest computer. 'It still works!' he says, his voice flat and loud in the unmoving space.

'It's just the last twitches of the nerves, love,' says Mum.

But even when the temperature drops and we have to wear all of our clothes at once to keep warm, the screens stay bright. We don't understand it.

'I think she's still here,' says my brother. 'It's the only explanation for why the computers still work.'

'Yes, that must be it,' I say, although I don't believe it.

The walls of Grandmother's body begin to thin. Soon they look like the drapes of a lacy shawl, and one day we wake up to the sight of her bones curving above us. We speak of leaving, but we don't want to miss the messages that have started appearing. Mostly they ask us if we're comfortable enough, or if we want more supplies – the kind of messages that Grandmother used to send when she was alive.

'It's some sort of glitch in the system,' mutters my brother. 'Something's gone wrong with the computer memory.'

Other messages begin. *My dears…* then a pause, followed by *…thick frost this morning,* or *…and she told me to tell you…* like fragments of half-heard conversations.

It's night the first time we see the sky through Grandmother's ribs. The moon makes her bones white, and the bare branches of the trees remind me of the patterns of her veins when she lived. Our neighbours' houses are dark, the streetlamps unlit. It's been a long time since we saw the outside world.

'We should try and survive outside,' say my parents, but there are eyes in the darkness, and teeth. The world is not for us anymore, say my brother and I. We will salvage plastic and cardboard to weave through our grandmother's ribs. We will live in the cathedral of our grandmother's bones.

The screen nearest to us flickers to life.

Dearests, Grandmother says.

Umeboshi

Eva Bohme

'As soon as I'm eighteen I'm moving back to England,' she said. 'Fact.'

I had guessed this would be Izzy's plan, but I asked her why, like I'd never imagined she would want to do such a thing. When I'd first met her, she'd told me that her parents were determined to live out the rest of their lives here in Japan. No more upheavals.

'She's not stupid,' I said to Tadashi, after Izzy had stood up and left the canteen, her meal only half finished.

It was Wednesday. Suiyōbi. The third day of Izzy's third week at school. Second term of senior high. Tadashi had been purposefully talking over me whenever I'd started translating the conversation he was having with my friends. They didn't know what to make of Izzy. I had no idea what she made of them. My friends. Classified as Nerds by the other kids. Identified by poor-to-average looks and a preference for computer games as a free-time activity. They called Izzy 'Nihongo ga hanasenai nihonjin'. The Japanese who can't speak Japanese.

Izzy was an only child with an English father and a Japanese mother. Born in the UK, she grew up in London then moved to Oxford, then Slough, and now here she was. Sixteen years old, living in Saitama city, and looking as bona fide Japanese as the rest of us, give or take a few flecks of green in her otherwise standard brown eyes. Only Izzy, full name Izumi Stephens, didn't consider herself to be

Japanese. She had only ever been exposed to English. English food, English TV and English conversation.

'Sorry, Hiro-chan, but she can't even introduce herself!' Tadashi's voice had taken the same tone that he used whenever he complained about his Science teacher, Mr Maki. Science was his weakest subject. Like me, he was more of a History and Arts kind of kid.

'Maybe she doesn't want to introduce herself to you. She introduced herself to me alright.'

'Yeah. In English.'

'Well it wouldn't hurt you to pause now and then so I can translate for her, would it?'

'No,' he said, 'I suppose it wouldn't hurt. But sooner or later, she's going to have to learn to speak.'

I passed him the soy-sauce as a peace gesture, but I had a sense that the invisible rope that had held Tadashi and I together as best friends since junior school had come untied.

One month after our first introduction, I was beginning to regard Izzy's refusal to speak the language as an act of defiance towards her parents. They had brought her here against her will. Tearing her apart from friends and forcing her to spilt with a boyfriend about whom I knew very little, because, she said, she 'didn't want to talk about him'. Izzy explained to me that her mum had insisted they move back to Japan to help to look after her elderly mother, Izzy's grandmother.

'She hates her,' Izzy said, 'but she needs to make sure her name is written in her will.'

It's true that Izzy introduced herself to me in English. She had no choice. Our homeroom teacher told her that I, Hiroaki, could speak English better than anyone else in the school. Then she informed us both that I would act as her 'mentor' while she settled in. I was in the drama club and I was also considered to be one of the best actors in the school, so I felt my appointed role suited me well.

Individual language lessons formed the bulk of Izzy's timetable. For regular classes she had a translator sitting with her. Izzy told me that she wished that it could always be me sitting with her instead. I closed my eyes and bowed my head to her. I'd never realised how lucky I was until I met Izzy. My mother had also married an English man. Black hair, dark eyes. You'd never have guessed I was hāfu by looking at me. Unlike Izzy's, my mother had taken the trouble to bring me up bi-lingual. We visited relatives in England every year and I could get by okay in either country. I felt bad for Izzy.

'Baka!' my classmates whispered to each other, staring at Izzy, while I translated the teacher's instructions. These kids thought she was stupid. Other kids thought she was arrogant. The former laughed at her, the latter admired her. Izzy seemed indifferent to it all. She never talked about how life at the school made her feel. As if she felt nothing. I wondered if perhaps her soul had been boxed away in England, along with the cases of clothes and books she'd left behind in her best friend's garage.

'So how come your mum didn't teach you Japanese as a child?' I'd put the question to Izzy during her first week at school, using my caring mentor voice.

'She's a selfish, lazy bitch. That's why,' she said. 'Fact.'

Secretly, I loved her lazy bitch mother for this. Imagine it. The prettiest girl in the school and I was the only one she spoke to. I'd gone from Nerd to Cool in three easy steps. Step one: The teacher appointed me as her mentor. Step two: She sought me out as often as she could during the school day and made no effort with any of the other kids, giving our pairing the prestige of exclusivity. Step three: All the Cool kids in the school started to notice her beauty and attempted to introduce themselves to her by acting as if they were friends with me.

When I asked Izzy why her parents hadn't sent her to an international school, she said her mother was punishing her for not being a boy. I guessed it was probably more to do with financial reasons, but I didn't say this to her.

One morning when Izzy arrived at school late, I said, 'I thought you were playing truant.'

'Too risky,' she said. 'Mum's threatened to home school me if I get kicked out.'

Our friendship in school had spilled over into post-school hangouts. The hangouts began when she realised that she needed my help with her homework. She would copy mine or ask me to type out her answers into Japanese. Without telling her, I improved on what she'd written. I also attempted to teach her some useful Japanese phrases. After repeating a phrase once, she'd say, 'This is boring. Let's watch a movie.' So movie watching became part of our post-homework ritual. Always her choice. Always in English.

'Weekends,' she said, 'are for cafes, shopping and cinema.' My friend Koji had invited me to join him and the others for the new *Spiderman* film, but I told him Izzy had already asked me to see it with her.

'But she won't understand it,' he said.

I considered telling him that we usually sat at the side in the 'empty seats zone' so that I could translate for Izzy without disturbing anyone. But then I realised how this would make me look.

'It's *Spiderman*. Dialogue's not important,' I told him.

'But you do everything with Izzy. We never hang out anymore.'

Koji was one of the Nerds. He was a good guy, but given the choice, I would always opt for Izzy.

'How did she even get into our school anyway?' he asked. I responded in the same way that Izzy had done when I'd put the question to her. I simply shrugged and changed the subject.

'So are you two an item, or what?' my friend Yasahiro asked me during our double-history class. We were studying the Edo period. Yasahiro had drawn a picture on my notebook of a couple holding hands. He'd labelled them Emperor Hiroaki and Empress Izumi.

'Not exactly but I think that's where it's heading,' I said.

'But. She's beautiful, isn't she?' he said, and then he repeated the adjective, looking out of the window, like he was addressing the trees outside in their full splendour of autumn.

Kireeeeiiiii.

He left his mouth open after letting the sound drift out, as if the word was still stuck there.

I decided it was better not to respond and started giving the teacher's monologue on the Boshin War my full attention.

It wasn't that the other kids didn't know English very well. We learnt new words and studied grammar every week at school. But we were never required to speak it. Those that tried to talk to Izzy were put off by the face she pulled if they got the pronunciation wrong or spoke too slowly. I told her she'd make a terrible teacher. I wondered how long she'd keep up her refusal to cooperate and if she'd get thrown out of the school. Izzy told me that as long as she did her homework, she would be allowed to stay. I didn't say it to her, but I thought that being expelled would be the best thing for her. I couldn't see her lazy mother carrying out her threat of home schooling. However, my role as mentor had been thrust upon me without choice. It was my duty to perform.

'How are you getting on in your language lessons?' I asked her one day.

'Not so great. My Japanese teacher is lazy,' she replied.

I noticed our class teachers had started to deal with 'the Izzy problem' by pretending she wasn't there. When she turned up with me at drama club, Mr Tanaka raised his eyebrows, and said, 'Izzy? Eh...?' When he addressed her in Japanese, she responded with the only native phrase I'd ever heard her speak in public, 'Igirisujin des. Nihongo wakaranai.' I'm English. I don't understand Japanese. Izzy took a seat next to me in the circle of chairs. Mr Tanaka scratched his head, then turned to me to ask me to translate for her as necessary. He gave her non-speaking parts and shared responsibility for the stage curtains.

'You know she could speak Japanese if she wanted to. How else do you think she made it past the entrance test?' Tadashi put the question to me over lunch one day. We were eating alone together because the girls had gone for a medical in the gym. The other Nerds were keeping their distance from me. I tried to change the subject, asking Tadashi about the latest *Dragon Quest* game instead. But he soon brought the conversation back round to Izzy.

'You should tell her how you feel. She must like you. She spends all her time with you.'

I knew Tadashi was right, but I was waiting for my moment. I was thinking Christmas could be the time. I would give her a gift and tell her I revered her above all other girls. The moment, however, announced its arrival well before the leaves had fallen, when Izzy issued an invitation which I regarded as 'privileged'.

It was Monday but Izzy was already planning her weekend.

'Do you want to come for a sleepover on Saturday? Dad says it's okay. We can drink shōchū. It'll be fun.'

Staying over and drinking alcohol. From that moment on I started thinking about what I would say to her after the right amount of shōchū had been consumed. During Maths and History, the teachers' lectures became background noise to the dialogue in my mind. Even as I was copying out algebraic formulae or facts about the Siege of Osaka, inside my head I was saying, 'Can I kiss you now? Can I hold you?'

At night, I forsook sleep and imagined the scenario unfolding perfectly. Like rehearsing for a part in the school play, I went over my lines again and again, only each time I said something different. Her response to me was always the same: 'I've been hoping this would happen.' Followed by kisses. Endless kisses that took me well into daylight when my throat started to tickle and my eyes started itching. I forced myself to stop thinking about her, imagined a cloudy night sky instead and managed three hours of sleep before school. And so it went on for the rest of the week.

'Hiroaki, you look tired. Are you sick?' Izzy asked me on Friday morning. If only she'd issued the sleepover invite today, I thought. A whole week of reduced sleep had been tough on my body.

'I'm fine. Let's do homework at mine tonight?'

There was no privacy at my house. My mother was always close at hand, offering us more snacks and checking we were

43

okay. Mum told me she loved having Izzy around. I think she thought of her as my girlfriend, but she never asked.

Saturday evening arrived and I started my walk over to Izzy's house, having spent the afternoon alone. I had opened up a novel and daydreamed my way through each page, kissing Izzy's cheek, mouth, neck, and taking none of the story in. Izzy had spent the day with her parents. It was their wedding anniversary. Tonight they would be going out with friends to celebrate and they wouldn't be back until after midnight. My bag clinked as I walked, the bottles of shōchū, bought with fake ID, bashing into each other as if they were trying to alert the police to my crime.

I suggested we should binge watch a comedy series that a friend in England had sent to me. Izzy was sceptical, but she agreed to give it a chance. A few minutes into the first episode, she was hitting her thighs and throwing her head back with laughter. Bakawarai. It's not that funny, I thought, but seeing her laugh like that made me want to watch all seven seasons. We made it halfway through Season One before we pressed pause to go outside to smoke cigarettes. When we came back in, she asked, 'What do you want to do now?' sitting herself down next to me on the sofa. 'Carry on watching?'

This is it, I thought. This is the moment. Desire overruled fear and I placed my hand on her thigh.

'Erm...' I said, directing my eyes towards her lips. 'Could I kiss you?'

I said the words quickly, quietly, as if I was hoping she wouldn't hear them, or if she did hear and she didn't respond, I could pretend I'd never said them. I wasn't even convinced myself that I had spoken the words out loud.

'You want to kiss me,' she said, repeating my request at full volume. 'Why?' She asked the question as if she'd never have imagined that I'd want to do such a thing. It was clear that she'd never thought about kissing me.

Me. One of the Nerds. Poor to average looks. Nothing to recommend me but my fluency in English. That's all it was. I saw it clearly when she took my hand off of her thigh and stood up and walked out of the lounge. She returned with two bowls of crisps and I trusted myself to the darkness of the room to hide my tears.

'We're just friends,' she stated.

Fact.

Spoken like a typed-up piece of History homework.

Fact.

No emotion.

No margin for discussion.

No double-spacing to leave room for comments.

Fact.

I poured some more shōchū into my glass, then passed the bottle to her. We continued to the end of the first season with her sitting on the armchair, while I remained on the sofa, feet up across the space she'd left empty.

Monday arrived and we carried on with our usual routines. Sitting together at lunch, talking about TV and making plans for the weekend. Nothing had changed on the outside, but underneath my ribcage, the soft flesh of my heart had started to toughen itself to leather.

After school we met at the gates as usual.

'Can we stop by at the mall on the way home?' she asked, while searching for the packet of cigarettes which I'd bought for her. I looked down at the pile of books, pens and cosmetics discarded from her bag on the ground where she crouched.

'Can't you go shopping by yourself now? You've been studying Japanese every day. I think you'll be okay.'

The words came out of my mouth as if I was spitting out food that I didn't like.

Umeboshi. Sour, with a hard pip at the centre.

Staring up at me, she started picking up each of the discarded items and dropping them back into her bag. Then she stood up.

'But you like shopping with me! Don't you?' she asked, in the same tone that she'd used with me when I'd requested to kiss her.

Did she really think that I'd enjoyed all those afternoons of standing around while she pored over jewellery and tried on dresses? I must have put on a great show. Truly I'd been worthy of the role bestowed on me as 'mentor'.

The coolest kid in our year walked past and smiled, nodding his head at me in approval. I buried my teeth into my bottom lip as I prepared to deliver the right combination of words in sweet, soft tones.

Strawberries, perfectly ripened.

Before I'd opened my mouth, Izzy spoke.

'Oh. I see,' she said.

Fact.

No room for discussion.

No comments in the margins.

Fact.

For the first time since we were introduced, she walked away from school without me.

Alien

Anna Chilvers

Poor kid, ending up here with me. He looks so much like his dad. What stupid bloody idiots we were, all those years refusing to be the one to speak first. I could have been there, seen him as a baby, seen him growing up. I could have got to know his mum, we might have been friends. When did I think we were going to have time if not then? What a waste. Too late now, now the kid's stripped raw and hurting. He thinks I hated his parents, I don't blame him for being wary. He looks so much like him. The way he brushes his hair away from his eyes, that's what his dad used to do. If I weren't such an ornery old bugger it might be enough to make me cry.

'Do you want to come UFO spotting at the weekend?'

Lucas looks at her face, trying to work out if she's making fun of him. 'UFO spotting?'

'It's one of the best places in the country for seeing them. There's a few of us going up Screw Hill. You can come if you like.'

'Have you seen any?'

'Not yet, but it's a laugh, we usually have a fire and have some beers.'

'Maybe the fire scares away the aliens.'

'I don't think a little human fire would scare them off.'

'Who knows? You don't know what they'd be like. They might be really tiny, smaller than the human eye can see.

They might be all around us. We might be breathing in aliens all the time.'

She stops laughing and stares at him. 'You're a bit weird you know.'

They're on watering duty. The hose has stuck, and he traces it back round the trestle tables until he finds the kink and unravels it.

'That should be okay now,' he calls.

When he returns Nina's got the spray on and the air is full of water. It's landing on the pelargoniums and begonias. Droplets of water pearl into balls in the centre of the leaves, then get bigger until they break into a runnel and stream down to the centre of the plant. The air is full of the scent of wet geraniums. He can't see her properly because she's got the light behind her and it's reflecting off all the water in the air, and it seems like she's an angel landed from a watery heaven.

'Houseplants next,' she calls out.

On the bus on the way home he holds a cactus in his lap. She had her bike tonight so she didn't catch the bus. He looks out of the window at the hills which crowd on both sides of the road, as though trying to shoulder each other out of the way. It feels as though the road and the bus and the line of houses could get crushed between them at any minute. He had a collection of cacti before, at home. He doesn't know what happened to them. Maybe they got sold with the house. The one he's holding is a notocactus. That name always made his mum laugh. 'Is it a cactus, or is it notocactus?' she would say, and there would be that tinkling sound she made when she cracked a joke, and his dad would groan. 'Not that one again.'

He wishes he'd chosen a different one now. Or a different plant entirely. The boss had said, 'Well done, Lucas, you've got through your first week. You may choose a plant as a welcome present. Up to six pounds fifty.'

He'd looked at Nina and she nodded. 'Everyone gets one. Either that or the sack. I got applemint – it's in our garden and it's spread everywhere.'

She didn't look too impressed when he chose a cactus. 'They're not very hardy,' she said.

'Oh, they are. They can withstand high temperature and months of no water. Years sometimes.'

'You do know this is Yorkshire, right? Have you not noticed the rain?' She strapped her cycling helmet on, and strands of her hair stuck out from under it. She blew at them to get them off her face, 'See you at school tomorrow.'

On the bus he mimics her, sticking out his bottom lip and blowing, so his breath is directed upwards across his face. His breath smells of liquorice.

He puts the cactus on his bedroom windowsill, then checks the compass on his phone. The window faces south-east, so it should get some sun. When he leaves for school in the mornings, the sun is still behind the houses opposite, but later it will rise above the rooftops and shine into his window.

'Good luck Notocactus,' he says. 'You and me both.'

Posh git with your posh accent coming up here with your money and your privilege, looking at my sister, don't go thinking anything mate, keep your slimy hands off her, I know what you bastards are like, you think you can look at anything and just have it, well not my sister, you go near her mate and you'll get my fist right where

*it hurts, you might have a la-di-da voice and a load
of money in the bank, but you can't just help yourself
to whatever you want you know.*

He's been at the school for six weeks now and he hasn't really spoken to anyone, not properly. After his first shift at the garden centre, he and Nina spoke briefly in the Sixth Form common room, about nothing much, the weather, what lessons they had that day. After she'd left, a boy said, are you from London then? Lucas started to explain that it wasn't really London, that it was just south of London and although the tube went out that far, it was actually … but the boy had stopped listening. He said, you sound right posh.

Lucas has thought about this a lot in the past few weeks. He's never thought of himself as posh. He went to ordinary school, not boarding school or anything. His mum and dad weren't rich. They lived in a semi-detached house on a cul-de-sac. They never said they were worried about money, but he thought they were probably just normal. His mum got the tube in each day, to an office where she did admin for a company that sold exotic plants. His dad was a nurse. But that's what everyone here seems to think of him. Posh, the posh London boy come to hang out in the North.

He'd asked his aunt about it. She said, take no notice, boy. Those that's worth knowing will take the time to know you, and those that don't, ain't worth knowing.

He wasn't sure about that. In theory it might be true, but on a day-to-day basis it meant that he had no friends. He sometimes messaged friends from his old school, but none of them really knew what to say. At least the people at school here didn't know anything about him. At least Nina didn't know.

He found out later that the boy was Nina's brother. He wondered about bringing it up that evening when they were loading petunias onto flatbeds, but he didn't want to spoil the moment.

'How's your cactus doing?'

'It's got some buds coming.'

'What, like flower buds?'

'Yes.'

'I didn't know cactuses had flowers.'

'Cacti. They have amazing flowers. Come and look.'

'We're meant to be sorting out these pots.'

'It'll only take a minute.'

They walk past the bedding plants and into houseplants. The cacti are in the far corner. Some of them have fake flowers and strangely coloured growths.

'Not those,' says Lucas. 'I don't know why they do that. Look, here.'

He noticed it yesterday. He always liked to drop by when he could, and he'd seen this Echinopsis flower was nearly ready. Today it's open completely, white and exotic, nearly as big as his hand.

'Bloody hell, that's amazing.'

'They don't flower very often, but when they do, they put everything into it.'

'Is yours going to do that?'

'Not like that. The flowers will be smaller, and not on a huge stalk like that. But they'll still be pretty amazing.'

'You know a lot about cactuses.'

'Cacti. Yes. I used to collect them. I had a greenhouse … before.'

'In London?'

Lucas puts out a finger and touches the white petal. It looks waxy, but feels like smooth and fresh, like a new leaf. 'We'd better get back to work.'

She catches the bus with him. 'My brother borrowed my bike, to go and see his new girlfriend. She lives out on a farm, miles from anywhere.'

At the bus stop she reminds him about the UFO spotting. 'It's this weekend. You should come.'

'Who are you going with?'

'A crowd of us.'

'From school?'

'Some from school, some not. It'll be fun.'

'I don't really know anyone.'

'You never will if you don't go out, dummy.' She nudges him in the ribs. He can still feel the pressure when they get on the bus. She sits next to him and talks. He couldn't say what she talked about. He is aware of the heat from her body close to his, the place on his side where her elbow had made contact. Maybe she's talking about people at work, or at school, names he's heard before but can't put to faces. No one has made physical contact with him since before, since London. His aunt is kind enough, but she's not the hugging sort.

Nina gets off the bus before him. 'So, what do you think?' she says as she rings the bell and stands up.

He nods, not sure if he's committing himself, or what to.

'Eight tomorrow night, at the canal bridge.'

When he gets in, he checks the cactus. There are seven buds in a circle. He thinks they're slightly bigger than they were yesterday.

'Are there UFOs here?'

On Saturdays his aunt doesn't go to work and she makes breakfast for them both. He'd like a lie-in, but he feels he has to make an effort. She's made a vegetarian full English, with homemade hash browns. He didn't know anyone made their own hash browns.

'Some folks think so. Why, have you seen one?'

He laughs. 'I've been asked to go UFO spotting, on the moors. I didn't know if it was a joke.'

'An excuse more like. We used to go, when we were teenagers, me and your dad and all our mates. We never saw any UFOs, but we had a lot of fun. When are you going?'

'Tonight.'

'I'll make you a batch of flapjack. It gets chilly up there at night.'

He chews a mouthful of vegetarian sausage. It's dry and doesn't taste of very much, but he keeps going and swallows. 'Why did you and dad stop speaking?'

His aunt looks up sharply, then her face softens. 'It was nothing really. Stupid when you think ... you imagine you've got all the time in the world, that one day you'll sort it out ... if I'd known...'

'Was it because he went to live in the South?'

She frowns. 'No, nothing like that. What a strange thing to think.'

He puts a forkful of mushrooms into his mouth. They're slimy and slip around on his tongue. He catches them with his teeth and bites, releasing the juice.

'It was about a girl I was seeing. Your dad thought she was bad news, and I got it in my head that it was because she was a girl. We had a big row. It turned out in the end that he was right, but I never told him. Pride and stubbornness.

53

Stupid to keep it up for all those years. I was only with the girl for six months.'

'Mum always said Dad was stubborn.'

'Runs in the family.' She looks into his face as if trying to detect stubbornness in his features. 'Doesn't do any good in the end.'

At eight he's waiting at the bridge, but there's no one there. He has a rucksack holding his aunt's flapjacks in a Tupperware box, and a four-pack of beer. It must have been a trick. He wonders if there are people watching, from a window, or behind the trees in the park, laughing at him waiting. He'll give it ten minutes then he'll go back, creep in the back way quietly and hope his aunt doesn't notice. He could spend the night drinking beer and stuffing his face with flapjack in his room.

'Hiya!'

It's Nina, and she's on her own.

He looks behind her and along the tow path. 'Aren't the others coming?'

'We're meeting them there. I told you silly, weren't you listening?'

'Oh, okay.'

They set off up a steep path on the other side of the bridge, across a field and into woodland. Lucas still hasn't got used to the ridiculous gradients. He'd thought he was fit enough – he used to run, cycle, swim – but these hills make him breathless. Nina is ahead waiting for him on a track at the top of the woods.

'Come on you, big softie,' she says, when he gets within earshot.

The track is comparatively level, cutting at an angle across the slope of the hill. As they walk, Lucas gets his breath back. Nina offers him a bottle of water and he takes a swig.

'Your brother called me a softie,' he says. 'A posh softie Southerner. I don't think he likes me.'

'Oh, don't take any notice of him. He's just cross with our dad.'

'Your dad?'

'Yeah. Mum doesn't help. She just goes on and on about people from London, and Jack just doesn't want her to think he's like Dad, so he goes too far the other way.'

'What did your Dad do?'

There's a stile at the side of the path and Nina climbs over it. 'This way.' The path runs diagonally across a field which is bordered by drystone walls. Sheep stare at them malevolently, then run away as they get near. The gradient has increased again. Nina waits for him in the far corner, next to some wooden steps over the wall.

'My mum had a business – mostly online – making candles and creams and stuff – she's a trained aromatherapist. Well this company in London that does the same sort of stuff, but huge, like they send stuff all over the world, they started targeting her. Like every line she came up with, they did something almost exactly the same, and they had more money for advertising – and basically they stole all her customers, then they offered to buy her out.'

'How was that your dad's fault?'

'It wasn't. But he met the woman who did it. He had to go to London anyway, and he said he'd go and talk to her – this was before they bought Mum out. Anyway, he had an affair with her, then he left and went to live with her in London.'

Nina climbs the steps and Lucas follows. The path stretches across another field.

'Race you.' She doesn't wait for an answer, but starts running. Lucas hasn't run for ages. It feels good to test the power in his legs. This is difficult, uphill with the beer and flapjack bouncing on his back, but halfway across the field he overtakes her, and it's him that reaches the next stile first and collapses on the ground, the breath burning his lungs.

Nina laughs at him. 'You should try fell running, you'd be good at it.' She's barely broken a sweat. On the other side of the stile is open moorland, with a thin path across it. 'We're nearly there.' She sets off at a pace.

He can't see anything or anyone other than a couple of sheep, and the moors seem to stretch in every direction, so he doesn't understand how they can be nearly there. Then he sees there's a dip where the path vanishes down a slope. As they get nearer the view opens up and he gasps. There's a lake – or is it a reservoir up here? – its water reflecting the setting sun. There's a beach too, small and rocky, and thronging with people. Twenty, maybe thirty people, sitting in groups or standing. There's a small fire on the shingle, and someone is cooking burgers on a barbeque.

'This is amazing!'

'I told you you'd like it.'

'Is that someone swimming?'

'Oh, that will be Jack. He always has to swim, even when no one else is.'

'Isn't it cold?'

'Yeah, pretty cold. Though this is the best time of year, after it's had all summer to warm up.'

Lucas shivers.

'Come on, let's get some food.'

Later, much later, Nina and Lucas are lying on their backs

on the moor looking up at the stars. The party is still going on down at the beach. Someone has brought music and people are dancing next to the water. The sound floats up the hill. The beer and flapjack are all gone.

'Look, there's one,' says Nina.

'That's a satellite.'

'How do you know?'

They watch quietly for a while. A sheep calls and is answered. Someone laughs down by the beach, then others join in.

'Shooting star,' says Lucas.

'Make a wish.'

There's so much he could wish for, but most of it is impossible. He can't turn back time, he can't make things different than they are. He wishes that the buds on his cactus will all open and that he gets a chance to show them to Nina.

The sheep has come nearer, they can hear its feet rustling the heather, its snuffling breath.

'Don't worry about my brother,' says Nina, 'he'll get used to you. It's not you he's angry with.'

I'm going to kill him. How dare he. It's not like he's in charge of me or something, just because we're twins it doesn't mean he can make my decisions for me. And what a fucking idiot, swaggering about and throwing punches, I wonder if he realises he just looks like a thug. I'm embarrassed to be related to him. I hope Lucas doesn't have a black eye tomorrow. I suppose I'm going to have to talk to Mum, and that won't be easy, but I'll have to get to her before Jack does, make sure he doesn't give her some skewed version.

Lucas can feel the pulse throbbing in his cheekbone. It's definitely swelling up despite the cold beer can Nina has given him to hold against it. 'I think it was just his way of making friends.'

Nina looks at him. He turns his head and they're looking into each other's eyes, then they both start to laugh. Lucas feels it start in his throat, but it claws hold of him, gripping his belly so he can't stop, and both of them are holding on to themselves and rocking from side to side breathless. The sheep baas in disgust and moves away.

Nina grabs hold of his arm and points at the sky.

'Look,' she gasps.

It's not shaped like a saucer, or glowing with flashing lights. It's dark and huge and it's hovering above them. Lucas doesn't feel scared, but the laughter leaves him, and the sad knot in his belly unravels, spreads through the whole of his body. He reaches out with his arm, but the thing is high up in the sky. After a minute it leaves, shooting off fast towards the stars.

The night seems terribly quiet. There are still noises floating up the hill from the party, but they seem far away.

'It felt like they were saying something,' Nina whispers.

'I think it was goodbye,' says Lucas.

He feels the warmth of her fingers as they touch his in the grass.

A Day of Rest

Melody Clarke

Sunday was a day of rest: he knew that. On Sunday, there were bounden duties that must be fulfilled, traditions that must be most solemnly observed; most of them, he reflected, revolving around honouring thy father and thy mother. Elbows on the windowsill, chin in cupped hands, he stared defeatedly at the back garden, with its new, green-metal monument to the Sabbath.

At sixteen, everything was too delicate for Matthew. The lawn mower, rescued from the tip and half-arsedly mended by his dad between sessions at the King's Arms, was just another example. It shed weirdly specific shaped lumps of metal, but had no discernible effect on the knee-high grass and dandelions, when he had been bullied into 'cutting the lawn'. He had tried. The thing weighed a ton, and he hadn't complained – well not much – even when the roller, roughly gaffer-taped to the iron frame, came away and flung itself at his shin. It was going to bruise, he could feel it. The ritual call and response that ensued was the same as it was every weekend:

'Muuumm! It doesn't work!'

'Course it works!'

'There's something wrong with it – a bit fell off…'

'What's the matter with you? Why do you have to break everything? I've never known anyone so clumsy!'

'It's not my fault!'

The slamming door echoed, recalling Sunday afternoons as they were in the beginning, are now, and ever shall be.

Matthew's eyes crept across to next door's back yard. He wondered what their house must be like – certainly calmer and tidier than his own, judging by the yard. Chastely hidden at ground level by a stern, seven-foot fence anointed with creosote, from up here it lay spread in glory before his wondering gaze. Once, from this viewpoint, he had been blessed by the sight of Faith Wilson sunbathing in a bikini, and something had stirred in him. He was sure – almost sure – that she knew he had been watching. The thought made him feel nervous, as it always did. Today, a half barrel overflowed with black and gold pansies like oversized honeybees. They shivered delicately, touched by a light breeze. A young tabby stretched, rubbed her face against the doorstep and purred. Lacy items fluttered from a nylon line, bouncing and straining to catch every ounce of the thin, milky sun.

Above the traffic noise, Matthew could hear the shouts of the Rankin Road kids. If he looked sharp he should be able to get out to the park before Dad got back, belching beer fumes and throwing his weight around. He slipped downstairs like a ferret, over the road and away.

They were standing in a circle around one corner of the bottle smash. Ten, maybe a dozen of them, chanting at some game they were playing:

'Georgie Porgie, pudding and pie!'

Little George White from number five was standing barefoot in the middle. Tears tracked from his curiously oriental blue eyes down his round cheeks. His feet bled onto the tarmac.

'I ain't 'llowed!' he protested in heavy, snot-laden sobs, 'Me mum said!'

'Hear that?' hooted Kelvin King, 'Little Georgie ain't allowed!' He flicked his fag end at George. 'Come on – dance Georgie, dance!'

Matthew nodded at Kelvin. 'Alright?'

'Yeah, alright.'

'Still on your, er, holiday off school?'

'Ha! Oh yeah – holiday – that's right. Keeping an eye on me mum, you know… me dad's due home next month.'

Matthew pulled a small, battered pack of Old Holborn from his shirt pocket. 'Want a fag?' he offered, handing the crumpled foil package over. Kelvin took it, expertly rolled a cigarette, and tossed the tobacco back. Catching it, Matthew slowly knelt down and stuck a dog-eared Rizla paper between his teeth.

'Must be a bit shit without your dad there,' he observed, 'I suppose you end up having to keep everyone in order.'

Kelvin squatted down on the grass opposite Matthew and exhaled a thick stream of smoke through his teeth. 'Yeah, well – you know – someone has to give 'em a bit of discipline, know what I mean?'

He knew it was the right thing to do. Distracting people was the one thing Matthew was good at – all his school reports said so – and he had excelled this afternoon. One by one, the Rankin Road kids had gathered round to listen to his jokes and banter. They'd laughed as he improvised an imaginary meeting between David Cassidy and Ingrid from the Co-op; by the end of his raucous impression of Mr Flatley's stammering instruction on how to use the 'B-b-b-b … Bunsen b-b-b-burner,' one or two had been cheering. Out of the corner of his eye, Matthew had spotted George, forgotten, hobble-rushing home, plastic sandals clutched to his chest.

Later, in the warm, sticky evening, something wonderful began, just as Father Moore had promised would happen one Sunday, if boys made sure to always do what they knew to be right. Faith found Matthew as he pushed through the broken hedge into the front garden. A breathy voice emerged from the dusk-shadowed privet, and the soft air wafted the gentle scent of synthetic orange blossom to him. She stepped forward, a white dress bringing her form into focus against the dark foliage. 'You saved George!'

Matthew's face suddenly felt hot. 'No I never.'

'You did – I saw you get that bloody bully Kelvin off of him … I think you're really brave.' She put her hand on his bare arm. 'I'm lonely. Me Mum's gone out for the evening.'

A flurry of small moths circled and dipped above them as Matthew followed her through the gap between the over-grown shrubs. She took his hand and led him into the silent, unlit house, and up the scrubbed wooden staircase.

Some things were meant to be delicate. Some of them were too delicate to talk about if there were grown-ups or girls listening. You could only get them at Boots by waiting until Speccy Mick was in charge, and even then you might have to back off quickly if another customer came in. At St Gregory's Catholic Secondary Modern such items were referred to as 'immoral goods'. Matthew had bought some immoral goods at Easter, in a spirit of optimism. He'd tried one on for size at once – just to check – and had carried the remaining two with him ever since. It was possible, he supposed, that they were out of date; it'd be just like

Speccy to try and get him into trouble. Or maybe they'd been damaged by two hours every Wednesday afternoon in his school bag on the changing room radiators. He'd never read the packet but it wasn't inconceivable. Inconceivable – that was a good one! Perhaps there had been something wrong with the machine that produced them – you read about things like that in the papers, like that time Mr Flatley told them about, when all those women ended up with purple hair because they'd mixed up the chemicals wrong at the dye factory. He could think of hundreds of reasons it could have happened. It didn't mean it was his fault. And anyway, why should he have to worry about it now he was on his own, now it was nearly midnight, now everyone else was sound asleep?

Matthew sighed, dropped his bare feet onto the floor beside his bed, and tiptoed over to the open window. The air that drifted in felt cool, and brought with it the familiar smells of the estate in summer: diesel fumes, crushed grass, hot asphalt, and occasional lardy gusts of late night cooking – bacon, fish, egg. He rolled himself a cigarette and looked down again at the yard next door. In the moonlight the pansies, silver now, still rippled. From the road outside, someone walking by hiccupped, and smothered a giggle. Matthew inhaled deeply. He couldn't be sure, but he had a feeling that now, in the end, everything would turn out alright.

The Prisoner

Jean Davison

If it hadn't been summer I might've lasted longer. Not much though without water. If the conservatory wasn't at the back of the house overlooking a yard with high privets. If I hadn't left my mobile on the kitchen table. If I hadn't slipped the window key in my dressing gown pocket when locking up before bed.

If it wasn't for her, none of this would have happened.

At first I told myself don't worry. Surely not even Cassie would leave me locked in for long. I sat on the wicker sofa and leaned back on the pale-green cushions, almost enjoying the silence. I rolled up the sleeves of my blouse. Sun poured through the big window facing me. I shaded my eyes with my hand and watched a couple of sparrows splashing in the bird bath.

Time passed. No one came.

Towards mid-day the temperature soared as the sun blazed through the glass ceiling. My south-facing prison became an oven. Sweat trickled down my back. I longed for a tumbler of water. I struggled again with the door but it refused to budge. Banged on the window. Yelled. I picked up a chair but couldn't raise it above the wall below the sill and ram it at the window with enough force. Same with the oak coffee table. I kept resting and then trying again until, winded and exhausted, I had to give up. I curled up on the wicker sofa.

By the time darkness fell I was beside myself. The temperature had dropped a lot but I was desperate to pee and I had to squat in a corner.

The night was cool and I slept.

I woke in uncomfortable brightness and feeling so thirsty I could barely swallow. A devil with drums pounded inside my head and my stomach screwed up in cramp. Infernal buzzing in my ears. Baking in the sweltering mid-day heat. Sour stench. I took off my slippers and pounded the glass, yelling at it to break. Made no impression, of course it didn't. This was crazy. Terror shook my sweat-sticky body. I sank to my knees and sobbed dryly.

Cassie, how could you do this to me?

I watched birds splashing in water and envied them. A sparrow hopped on the window ledge. The outside world was so close and yet so far.

Drifting in and out of consciousness, I squinted at the dazzling light above. Covered my head and face with cushions. Tried to squeeze under the sofa but no room. No escape. Buzzing? A rescue helicopter that couldn't find me. Weak with hunger and craving water I searched on hands and knees for a spring. Crawling on sand. Waking. Crawling on vinyl. Barely able to stand.

Red. The colour of the back of my eyelids. Nothing else to see with eyes shut. Sound? Switched off. No buzzing in my ears. A whirlwind sucking me in. Lifting me up. Carrying me away from hunger, thirst and searing heat. Taking me to the calm. I was ready now and waiting. No longer afraid of death creeping up close. Death, smothering me in a red blanket and twirling me around. Death, red and silent.

'Sarah! Oh my God!'

Liz? No, this couldn't be my sister, screaming and shouting and shaking me. Not here in this red place. She couldn't come yet. I tried to say, shush, you'll waken the dead. But no words came. Just a faint squeak.

Next thing I was in a bed, propped up on pillows. Not red now. Dark. A shape holding a beaker to my mouth and cool water sliding down my throat. My head hurt and for most of my hospital stay I was submerged in nightmares of being locked in.

Back home to complete my recovery, I still slept a lot at first. Each time my eyes flickered, Liz was there, giving me Lucozade. She came with Cassie one day and brought her into my bedroom.

'Your aunt almost died,' Liz said. 'For God's sake, Cassie, you're fourteen, not four. You should've known. Now, what have you got to say to her?'

'Sorry, Aunty Sarah. I didn't think it'd end like this.'

Cassie? Send her away.

By the time I was ready to ask Liz what happened, I could remember it all, but I asked anyway, curious to hear her version.

Liz sat on the bed and sighed. 'It was a silly joke gone seriously wrong.'

'She's an idiot,' I said. 'She'll end up in prison one day.'

'I know it turned out awful, but she didn't mean any harm.'

I didn't buy it. Cassie was wicked. I closed my eyes and saw her again on that Saturday morning. She'd popped round to bring me a jam recipe from Liz and then asked to go to the bathroom. Next thing she was in the living room dancing to music with her ear buds in. She'd doubled up her skirt at the waist till she was nearly showing her backside.

'You're not going anywhere looking like that,' I said.

Cassie turned to me and grinned with glossy pink lips.

A fourteen-year-old made up like that was inviting danger. I knew it, so I had to stop her.

'Wash off that lipstick. Now.'

'You can't make me.'

'Give it to me.' My desire to confiscate it overwhelmed.

'Why? So that you can try to make yourself look pretty?' She gave me a pitying look. Pity? I didn't want her damned pity.

I pushed her forward from behind in what became a parody of a frog-march, with her giggling and taunting me.

I gasped. Us two in the mirror. Faces cold and hating. I imagined fractured glass: us disintegrating into unworthy and unloved pieces. I turned from our reflection and we got to the kitchen sink where I tried to rub her lips with a flannel. She grabbed it and shoved me away.

'Fuck you!' she said. 'How dare you assault me?'

I stormed through to the living room, clenching and unclenching my fists. She was trying to wind me up, so best to ignore her.

Instead of retaliating again she put on her coat, to my relief. I expected to hear the front door slam but, no, she was still around.

I waited a while and then went looking for her. She was in the conservatory, smoking. I grabbed her cig and while I was wondering where to put it, she skipped out and I heard the key turning. She grinned at me like a fiend through the small glass panel in the door.

And off she went.

'She thought your neighbour would soon let you out,' Liz continued. 'She knew Jackie pops in to see you regularly. She even pushed a note through her door saying: "Look in Sarah's conservatory."'

'So she says. I'll ask Jackie when she gets back from holiday. But, yes, no one came. Not until her ladyship decided to tell you. Not until it was almost too late.'

Liz gave a nervous smile and smoothed my bed sheets. 'When she told me, she'd no idea you'd be still locked in. She thought you were sulking. Soon as I heard, I rushed to my car and she ran after me, pleading to come.'

'Why? So she could spit on my dead body?'

Liz shook her head. 'Oh, don't be like that, Sarah. When she realised what she'd done and then saw how poorly you were, she was so worried and sorry.'

'Oh, yeah, I bet she was.'

'I believe her,' Liz said. 'She really is sorry.'

Rebel kids need disciplining for their own good. But Liz and Pete, her stepdad, let her get away with anything. She'd been spoiled rotten. When her parents had divorced, Jim, whom she always referred to as her real dad, went to live thirty miles away in Norwich and Cassie went wild. Hanging out with older kids who were a bad influence. Moody. Drinking. Drugging.

'No. No way. Absolutely not.' I folded my arms and leaned back in my comfy armchair.

Liz fiddled with the button on her cardigan. 'I wouldn't ask but we've sought other possibilities, tried among friends and so on but nobody's available so I thought ... well, you're family and we've no other options.'

Pete's mother, a widow living in France, didn't have long left after a drawn-out battle with cancer and they wanted to go and see her, leaving Cassie with me.

Even before, I wouldn't have been happy about it. Never could stand the bloody kid. But now, after all she'd put me through, no way would I let her set foot in my house ever again.

'You could take her with you.' I looked at Liz questioningly and added, 'If you really wanted her there.'

'We'll take her for the funeral but it's best if just the two of us go to be with Sophie now. She's asking to see us both before she dies. Pete's her only son and she sees me as the daughter she never had.'

I shook my head. 'Yes, I know, and I'm really sorry, but…'

A woman pleading on her death bed. What could I do? And I'd found out from my neighbour, Jackie, that Cassie really had pushed the note through her door. My resolve was weakening.

'You're right. I shouldn't be asking you,' Liz said. 'Of course it won't work. You and her together. I don't know what I was thinking of.'

I bristled. Did she think I couldn't manage?

'No, it's me being selfish,' I said. 'I could look after her for a few days.'

Liz stared out of the window. 'No, it wouldn't be right after what happened.'

'It'll be fine. I just needed time to get used to the idea. I don't mind. Honestly.'

So there I was on Saturday with Cassie, waving off Liz and Pete. A sickly feeling twisted my guts as their taxi disappeared round the corner. I dreaded the days ahead but I would make an effort.

'Come on, Cassie,' I said. 'How about us going for fish and chips at Friar Tuck's?'

She shrugged.

Cassie chased chips around her plate with her fork.

She was pretty. I had to give her that, with her long red hair, beautifully soft and shiny. She was too thin in her clingy black T-shirt and tight jeans, her wide strapped watch hanging loosely on her wrist. Her pale face had taken on a slightly gaunt look, which I found alarming. Her big dark-brown eyes held a lost and lonely expression, causing a strange warmth to well up inside me; an icicle melting. As we sat, just the two of us facing each other across the table, it struck me that maybe this was the first time I'd actually looked at her properly, never mind felt for her.

'You need to put on some weight,' I said. 'Are you on one of those silly diet fads?'

'Course not. I'm not hungry right now, that's all.' She put down her knife and fork.

'Come on, Cassie, you need to eat more. You've hardly touched your fish.'

'What's it to you?'

'I'm worried about you,' I said, surprising myself with the truth of my statement.

'You? Yeah, right.' She flushed and looked down at the table, giving a sceptical laugh. I'd never seen her look embarrassed before. 'I've heard my mum say that, but then what did she do? I can't believe she and my stepdad went to France without me.'

'It won't be for long and they do care about you. We all do.'

'Oh yeah, I can see that.' She laughed but her eyes glistened. 'I've got some mates who live in a squat. That's where I want to go, but I think even they don't want me with them either.'

'Living in a squat wouldn't be much fun.'

'Yes it would. I need to be free.' She shot me a quizzical look. 'Did you ever want to run away?'

I nodded. 'Yes, at your age. But that's not freedom. Wait till you're a bit older.'

'How can I make it 'til then?'

'We can work it out.'

'That's in a Beatles song. See, I know more than you think.'

'Maybe we both do.'

We looked at each other and smiled.

I thought we'd made a breakthrough. I really did, especially when before she went to bed that night, she said, 'About locking you in. I shouldn't have done it. I'm sorry.'

'No, you shouldn't have. Look how dehydrated I was.' I reached out my hand to her. She stiffened. I withdrew. Best not to rush it.

'You wouldn't understand,' she mumbled.

Next day at breakfast she was quiet. She picked up her coffee but before she'd taken a sip, her mobile rang and she left the room to answer it. I heard her footsteps going upstairs. Her coffee and porridge went cold.

She spent most of the day in her room. During the little I saw of her, she was either on her phone, or hanging around, sullen and moody. She ate hardly any of the stew I made for our tea and sat at the table with her headphones on listening to music.

She left her bowl on the table, not staying to help with washing up, and went upstairs. When she came down, she'd changed from jeans into a short black dress and red high heels. Her face was plastered in make-up.

My stomach muscles tightened. Oh no, here we go again.

Scarlet lipstick looked ridiculous on one so young, but the black eyeliner and mascara made her look at least eighteen. A worldly eighteen.

'Where do you think you're going like that?'

She grinned. 'Out.'

I couldn't help my temper rising. 'Out? And is that what you want to look like when you go out? Is it? A cheap tart?'

A distant memory. My dad calling mini-skirted me that.

'Better than looking like you do with all that flab,' Cassie said. 'I'd hate to be you.'

She turned and headed for the door.

'Now you listen to me, young lady.'

'Fucking fat cow!'

My heart was beating fast. I didn't know how to deal with her. But she was fourteen. I couldn't let her get the better of me. I rushed to the door and blocked her way. 'You're going nowhere.'

'You can't stop me. You can't hold me here against my will.' She grinned. 'Just you try it. Go on then. Try it. I dare you.'

We glared at each other.

She marched to the back door next to the conservatory entrance. I followed. Her mobile rang. She pulled it out of her bag and dropped it when I tried to confiscate it. As she stooped to pick it up, I grabbed her by the shoulders and shoved her into the conservatory. Caught off guard, and tottering in those silly heels, she didn't struggle much. The key was in the keyhole, tempting me. I locked her in. Her startled look as she peered through the door told me she hadn't expected me to stand up to her. She had thought she held all the power.

She banged on the door. 'Let me out! You can't do this! Fuck you! Fuck you! Fuck you!'

I left her mobile on the floor, and smiled. She could stay there for a while to simmer down.

'I'm off out,' I called to her. 'See how you like it in there.'

I'd make a quick visit to Morrison's down the road and be back to let her out. I'd only be gone fifteen minutes but it might teach her a lesson. Get her to reflect on her attitude.

At the supermarket I flung a few things carelessly into my basket, fumbled at the till for my money and nearly left my purse on the counter. Outside, I started crossing the road, eager to get back. I was still so preoccupied with Cassie that I didn't see the red mini until I heard a screeching of brakes.

'Concussion,' the nurse explained when I woke, touching the bandage on my head. 'You got run over on the road opposite Morrison's.'

A young doctor with a notebook appeared at my bedside.

They asked lots of questions to test my brain. Asked my name and address. Asked who my next of kin was. I told them Liz, but she was away.

My head was fuzzy. I drifted away into a dream in which I was back locked in the conservatory. Or someone was. Not sure who. Must be me. The world turned red and this time I resisted being dragged out of the calm.

But the room spun and it was a hospital ward. 'What's wrong with me?'

'Head injuries but it seems nothing too serious. We'll keep you in for a few more days of observation and tests but don't worry, you're doing fine. When your sister's back we can start thinking about your discharge.'

I knew my memory wasn't right. I couldn't quite grasp something on the periphery. 'Wait. There's something else,' I said. 'I can't think what it is.'

Next, I was having a full-blown panic attack. I clutched the blankets and gasped. 'Help, I can't breathe. I'm scared.' I tugged at the doctor's sleeve. 'You've got to do something.'

I was aware my voice had risen hysterically and the doctor's eyes narrowed with concern.

By the time I calmed down, I was bone tired.

'There's something I need to remember,' I murmured as I sank into sleep.

Sedation was a wonderful thing. I think that's what they did to me over the next few days. I felt pleasantly woozy and I slept a lot.

The temporary calm ended abruptly one day with Liz almost dragging me out of bed. 'Where's Cassie? Where is she?'

'Cassie?'

'We called at your place in the taxi on our way home. The lights were out and no one answered the door. We kept trying to get you or Cassie on your mobiles.'

'Mine's switched off in my bedside locker. I can ring but we're not supposed to.'

'And then back home there's this answerphone message from you saying you're in hospital after getting run over and telling us not to worry.'

'That's right. Nothing to worry about. The doctor thinks I'll be fine soon.'

'But they say you've been in here since last week with memory problems and confusion. Cassie was staying with you. Where is she?'

'Staying with me?' I thought hard. The weird dream I'd had sprung into focus. 'The conservatory. Trapped. Who? Me? Or someone else? Us?'

'What?' Liz's eyes widened in horror.

'Oh, it's nothing. I was just remembering a confusing dream where things got mixed up together. Dreams are often like that, aren't they? Make no sense.'

What on earth was the matter with Liz? She practically dragged Pete out of the ward.

I sat up, a memory returning in an explosion of fear. 'Oh my God!'

I got out of bed and was fumbling frantically for my clothes in the locker when the doctor appeared.

'Miss Thomas, are you all right?'

'I'm going,' I said.

'I wouldn't advise it.'

'You can't stop me. You can't keep me here against my will.' I almost added, 'Fuck you!'

'Please calm down, Miss Thomas. Why don't you wait 'til your sister gets back?'

'I'm wicked. Wicked.'

He shook his head and a puzzled look formed on his face. He was probably thinking, send for a psychiatrist, this woman's off her trolley.

I cleared my throat and made an effort to speak calmly to put his mind at ease. 'Doctor, I have to tell you this. I think I've murdered my niece.'

They urged me to get back in bed. My legs went wobbly and I realised I wasn't yet strong enough to leave. There was nothing I could do to help so I might as well wait for news. News. What news? Supposing Cassie was lying on the brown vinyl floor. Dead. I'd never forgive myself for being stupid enough to lock her in.

'I've been an idiot all my life,' I told the nurse. 'Everyone used to say I would end up in prison one day.'

Liz and Pete returned. Liz's face was white. 'We've reported Cassie missing to the police,' she said.

'Missing? Wasn't she in the conservatory?'

'She smashed a window,' Pete said. 'With a chair, I think. Got through into the house.'

Relief washed over me. Thank goodness she'd found more strength than I had.

'So she must be okay,' I said. 'But where is she?'

'We don't know,' Liz said, tearfully.

'Was her mobile on the floor by the back door?'

'No, but she's not answering it. We phoned her friends, tried Jim too, anyone we could think of, and no one's seen or heard anything of her.'

'She's punishing me,' I said. 'That's what this is about.'

'For God's sake, Sarah, this isn't about you. Her school friend said she used to talk about hitch hiking to Norwich to live with Jim.'

'Hitch hiking? Oh, God, no. That's dangerous,' I said.

'Exactly, and you should know. She's not the kind of girl to sit for long waiting to be rescued, is she? So she's been away a few days now. She could be anywhere. Anything could have happened.' Liz was trembling and sobbing. 'For God's sake, Sarah, why did you lock her in? Revenge, eh? Well, that's sick. You're an adult and she's a child.'

I clutched my stomach. The guilt and fear were overwhelming. Tears rushed down my cheeks. I hated myself.

'Liz, love, don't.' Pete said. 'This isn't the time for anger or blame.'

Liz leaned on Pete's shoulder and he finished off the story.

'Anyway, we called the police,' Pete continued. 'We're going to the station now.'

The police visited me in hospital later that day and I told them all I knew. I'd no idea where Cassie was. I pictured her living with druggies and dropouts in a squat, but where was that place? Worse still, what if she'd climbed into some maniac's van? Cassie, pretending to be tough. Cassie, believing herself to be invincible. Cassie, a fourteen-year-old in a short black dress, thinking she was grown up. Me, at her age. I did it all. Yes, and I fell into danger. My body was shaking at the memory. At least I survived. A lump rose in my throat. Stirrings of tenderness and warmth. Dislike overpowered by love for two children who'd lost their way.

I rang her mobile. No reply. Desperation prompted my repeated dialling. More than anything else I wanted her to be safe. Even wanted to hear her saying 'fuck you' and calling me a fat cow. Only she could end this nightmare. Please let her be all right. I tapped in her number yet again and pressed my mobile to my ear, willing her to answer.

Somewhere there was a phone that kept ringing and ringing.

Dancing on Ice

Trina Garnett

Penny wanted to turn the heating up; Richard wanted it off. It was late September, three days after their wedding anniversary, and there was a chill in the air.

'It's nineteen degrees – look,' said Richard, pointing to an app on his phone.

'Well it's bloody freezing.' Penny pulled the sleeves of her jumper over her hands and covered her mouth. They watched TV in silence: a Scandi drama. A lone detective stumbled out of her car into a snowstorm.

'We could always light the candles?' suggested Richard, nodding towards the hearth.

'Very funny.'

The fireplace had been a point of contention ever since they moved in. Penny had ripped out the old electric fire and replaced it with vanilla-scented candles and fairy lights. Not practical but pretty. That's what Richard used to say about her too.

She sighed and watched her breath hang in the air like a tiny cloud before disappearing.

Penny called the heating company the next morning.

'All of our advisors are busy,' said the automated voice. 'If you are calling about your bill, press one. If you have a problem with your heating, press two. If you have a problem with your relationship, press three...'

Penny let the voice cycle through the options again, her

finger hovering over the keypad.

'If you have a problem with…'

She pressed three and the voice continued.

'If you're thinking of leaving, press one. Or, stay on the line if you'd like to speak to an advisor.'

The hold music had barely kicked in when a male voice answered. 'Hello?'

'Hi,' said Penny. 'I'm calling about my husband.' She stopped. That's not what she meant to say at all. 'I mean heating. Not husband; heating.'

'How did you get this number?' The voice sounded annoyed. 'This is an internal department. You'll have to hang up and call again.'

'Can't you transfer…?'

The line clicked and went dead. When Penny rang back the options had changed.

The heating complaints department was more helpful. 'We'll send an engineer out this afternoon,' said the woman. 'Is there anything else I can help you with today?'

'Yes, when I rang earlier there was an option for relationship advice,' said Penny. She felt foolish now she'd said it out loud.

The woman laughed.

'Sorry, love, we're only a heating company. We're not miracle workers!'

The heating engineer was a young lad with kind eyes and violent tattoos. Very polite.

'You've got permafrost in your living room,' he said. 'That's what's confusing the system.'

'Permafrost?'

'Yes, look.' He rolled back the carpet to reveal a thick

layer of ice in front of the fireplace the size of a large coffee table. Below the surface were shadows and shapes of things she couldn't quite make out.

'You'll need to keep the heating on permanent for a couple of days,' he said. 'When the ice starts to melt just mop it up, like de-icing a fridge.'

'Is this…' Penny struggled to find the words. 'Usual?'

'Oh yes, it's quite common.'

He nodded at the anniversary cards on the mantelpiece. 'How many years is it?'

'Seven,' said Penny, smiling.

He nodded.

'Well good luck,' he said. 'Sometimes the ice can be … tricky.'

Before he left, he attached a sensor to the living room wall.

'What's that for?' asked Penny.

'That's just so head office can monitor the temperature remotely,' he said.

'Permafrost?' said Richard in disbelief when he got home. 'How the bloody hell has that got in here?'

He looked at her as though she'd let it in with the cat.

'I don't know. He said we have to keep the heating on.'

Richard switched on the TV and there was a loud bang. The screen went black.

'Oh, for Christ's sake!'

The ice had started to melt.

'I'll get a bucket,' said Penny.

In the kitchen Penny found herself wondering what she would have said if she'd got through to an advisor.

Someone once asked if she was happily married and she

surprised herself by not knowing what to say. It was at an awards ceremony she'd gone to with work. She was ordering drinks when a man at the bar talked her into buying a cocktail she hadn't tried before. The cocktail was stronger than she was used to and had a rude name.

Later, after the awards were handed out, he found her again and asked if she was enjoying her 'Triple Orgasm'. She was just drunk enough to laugh – at the situation as much as the question.

He was called Steven. No not Steven, Stefan. His mother was German. He told her she'd died in a skiing accident when he was a teenager. She remembered that about him. Penny told him she didn't have any children but had once been pregnant with twins. It's funny what you'll say to a stranger that you don't tell the people closest to you. She tried to picture him but couldn't remember if his eyes were blue or green, his hair blonde or brown. He smelled of expensive cologne and his mouth had tasted of cherries.

There was a scratching sound at the back door. Penny opened the door to let in Ratface. That's what Richard nicknamed her. They didn't know her real name or who she belonged to.

Penny had taken to buying tins of cat food 'just in case'. She forked out some tuna into a bowl while Ratface slunk past her.

'You're too soft with that cat,' said Richard. He was in one of his disagreeable moods. He reached across her to pour himself a whisky.

'She's not doing any harm. How was work?' she asked. He answered in detail about a project he was working on which was or wasn't going well.

Her thoughts drifted back to the night of the awards do. She sometimes wondered how things might have turned out differently. If she'd replied to Stefan's text…

There was a yowl from the living room. Penny got to the door first and pushed it open. She saw Ratface soaking wet carrying something limp in her mouth that she dropped at Penny's feet.

'Is it dead or alive?' asked Richard.

Penny could only stare at it.

The toy elephant was blue and made of felt. She recognised it instantly though she hadn't seen it for years.

'Penny?'

She turned her head towards him but in her mind she was back at the hospital on the day of the scan, standing in front of a charity stall selling homemade crafts. Richard was on his final tour in Afghanistan and she was dying to tell someone the news.

The woman at the charity stall was delighted for her.

'Twins?' she said. 'That's going to be double trouble!'

Penny planned to surprise Richard, tell him in person, when the time was right. She wasn't one hundred per cent sure how he'd take it. But by the time he came back there were no twins. There seemed no point in mentioning it, no point making him miserable too.

'Penny?' said Richard. 'Whatever it is we can sort it.'

The ice by the fireplace had all but melted, with just a few chunks of ice floating like icebergs. The water was so murky it was impossible to say how deep it was.

'What's all this stuff in here?' said Richard, crouching at the edge of the water and rolling up his sleeve. He plunged his arm in and swirled the water around. A whisky bottle bobbed to the surface.

'Where's all this rubbish coming from?'

'There's something inside it,' said Penny.

'Ha – a message in a bottle!'

Richard picked it up and tried to shake out the piece of paper. As it unfolded Penny saw it was a photo of Richard as a boy dressed in camouflage trousers and green knitted tank top aiming a toy gun at the camera.

'Aww look at you there!' she said, reaching for a better look.

Richard hurled the bottle against the fireplace and Penny jumped as the glass smashed against the cast iron. The photo floated face down onto the water.

'What did you do that for?'

Richard shook his head.

'I just wanted to see what you looked like,' said Penny.

'It wasn't me.'

'Well who…'

'My brother.'

'I didn't know you had a…'

'I don't.'

His tone silenced her questions.

'I told you not to turn the bloody heating on!' he said. She could always tell when he was angry because his left eyebrow started twitching.

The sensor on the wall glowed red.

'Thank you for using Emote heating,' said the automated voice. 'You have reached the optimum temperature.'

Richard ripped the sensor from the wall and threw it into the water where it fizzed and sank out of sight.

'I'm turning it off again until we get this sorted.'

Penny nodded, wrapping her arms around herself, anticipating the chill.

'Sorry for shouting,' said Richard.

Penny found herself crying. How silly to cry now he was apologising.

'Hey, hey, no need for that,' he said, drawing her towards him. She breathed into the fabric of his jumper, feeling her own breath warming her face. From the muffled sound of the TV she could hear music that sounded familiar.

'Do you recognise this?' whispered Richard.

'Our wedding song,' she said.

He started to sway in time with the music and she followed him.

'Seven years ago,' she said. It seemed so long ago and yet not long at all.

'Seven years and four days,' he corrected.

'Do you still remember our dance?'

They had stumbled through it on the day and they stumbled through it again now, sloshing through water that was already freezing over. By the end of the song they were laughing.

'Don't worry,' said Richard. 'We'll get this mess cleared up and buy a new carpet. It will look just as it did before. You'll never be able to tell what happened.'

Background Music

Andrea Hardaker

Looking back, I'm not sure whether it was a gradual thing or if it just sort of 'happened' overnight.

Whatever it was I didn't notice it fully until one of those early northern mornings when the sun hangs low in the sky, limp and wilting.

I had nipped into the garden to hang out some washing, determined to make the most of the dry weather. It was possibly the last time I'd get the chance to hang stuff out, without the definite possibility of rain (there was always a strong chance in Yorkshire, but at least at this time of year you could be guaranteed a few dry hours here and there.)

It was nearing the end of September. Summer had spent the past few weeks gathering up her belongings, making sure she left no trace of her annual visit. The leaves were already glowing red and gold and I knew that just around the corner, an autumn wind was gathering force, waiting to blow them all out like candles, leaving us once again in the dark.

Despite the early morning sun, there was a slight chill in the air so I wasn't keen to linger, but I was distracted by a creeping sensation that something was missing. I stopped and glanced around. I couldn't for the life of me understand what it could be – everything in the garden looked normal. The grass, the flowers, the shrubs were exactly where they should be. I could even smell the sweet scent of basil from the herbs I'd proudly grown over the past few months when I'd thought the world was going to end and food might become a scarcity. I shivered at the memory and pulled my cardigan tight across my chest.

A flock of birds swooped overhead, like a shadow blocking out the sun. The unease heightened. Something wasn't right. What was it? The sun? The breeze? The air? God forbid it was the air. I hurried back inside, pulling the door hard behind me. It had been a strange few months, stranger than anything I'd experienced in my entire life. We had been living out our days as if we were playing a part of some sort of horrific sci-fi movie. One where the life-sucking alien was invisible, rendering us all useless in the fight. Like that film from the seventies, *The Body Snatchers*, where the aliens (cunningly disguised as houseplants) stole the bodies of people and replaced them with doppelganger aliens.

Whenever the 'alien beings' saw a real human they would screech loudly and point to show the world where the danger lay. That was what it felt like; this virus that was keeping us all apart from each other, all afraid of each other. Surely things couldn't actually get any weirder?

But that feeling … that intuition … was still with me, even when I stepped inside.

Tom was already up, sat at the kitchen table with his back to me. He tended to skip breakfast, fattening himself instead on the perpetual feed of his iPhone. He had his earphones wrapped tightly round his head giving him that 'plugged in' look. But as I entered, he must have sensed some movement because he turned to me, his eyes blazing.

'Am ot meer ng a u-ng ask – o atter ot ey ay.'

I rubbed my ears. 'What?'

He stared at me. 'Ah ed, am ot meer ng a ask – o atter ot ey ay.'

I had no idea what he was saying – he was literally talking

gobbledygook – as if he had his mouth full of chicken. Whatever he was going on about, I could tell he was annoyed. 'What was it now?' I wondered. The neighbours' kids making too much noise playing out in the street? HimNextDoor cutting his grass too early? Or was it something he'd sucked in from his Twitter feed?

'Jesus,' I said, 'take off your headphones, you idiot! I can't make out a word you're saying.'

'Ot?' he said, removing them, rubbing his ears.

I sighed, too tired to continue the conversation. We hadn't been getting on too well recently. It could be Lockdown, I thought, after all we have been stuck with each other's company for the past few months. But I couldn't help the suspicion that it ran deeper than that. We were arguing about everything these days – Lockdown, the NHS, Boris, Cummings, cases, staying in, going out, the economy, schools, toilet paper, food, his drinking, my smoking…

It had ended up with us pretty much living separate lives in the same house. We both went to bed wearing headphones, avoiding each other's eyes, staring at the world through a computer screen. We'd even started texting each other from the next room for God's sake!

I frowned at him. 'I'll speak to you later,' I said. 'Get back to your music, or … whatever.' I only realised I was yelling when I turned my back on him. My voice bounced back at me from the walls but even that sounded strange.

I took several deep breaths. No wonder I couldn't make out what he was saying. He had music blasting in his ears all day long. Surely any reasonable person knew it was a bad idea to play your headphones at full volume? It was bound to affect your hearing and therefore your speech. It was worse at night. Sometimes he had them turned on so loud

I couldn't sleep. It drove me crazy. But I was done warning him. If he was struggling to speak it was his problem. I had warned him, but, of course, he'd only argued back.

He seemed agitated. 'Ot? Ots ong iu. Ay oo eak ng ik a?'

I didn't answer. There was no point when he insisted on being like this. What the hell was he playing at? Typical. He'd gotten so childish recently. Shouting at the television set, yelling at people on Twitter, posting all sorts of strangely 'meaningful' icons on his Facebook feed that really meant nothing whatsoever if you knew him, I mean, if you really knew him. What a bloody hypocrite! But the fact was, he couldn't agree with me, I couldn't agree with him and neither of us seemed to agree with the world. How could we when the world was so obsessed with peoples' identity it had lost its own? It didn't take a genius to realise that the more people divided themselves up into tiny little categories, the less chance there was of real change ... but Tom and I couldn't even agree about that. We had a hole in the living room wall where his fist had been only a few nights back after an argument had broken out between us while we were watching the news. I was furious (after all it would be me that had to redecorate) until he pointed out that I had actually broken the remote control by lobbing it across the floor just a few weeks earlier. Personally, I didn't think that was as bad as punching a hole in the wall but whatever ... I shook my head and turned on the kettle.

It seemed to take ages to boil. Great, I thought. It's all steamed up but I didn't hear it boil. That's all I bloody need, a broken kettle. I lifted it up but before I could consider it any further, I felt Tom's hands on my shoulder and grimaced.

'U a eeng eely ange. Ots ong?'

Something fluttered inside my chest, like the beat of wings against glass. I glanced out the window at the garden, watched a bird swoop down from the trees, saw the arms of my washing flap frantically in the breeze as if trying to warn me of some imminent danger. I moved free of him and straightened my shoulders.

'I've no idea what you're playing at but it's getting on my fucking nerves – oh and you forgot to get milk. So *I'm* going to have to go get some.'

I dashed up the stairs to grab my purse and face mask. Could we not even get through a morning without a row? I could still feel his touch on my skin. A few months ago (perhaps longer) I'd have savoured the feeling. Now I felt oddly bruised, as if even the touch of him was too much.

I glanced at the time on my phone. If I got to the shops early, I'd avoid the queues. Out the corner of my eye I saw a notification. 'Don't look,' I told myself. 'Seriously. Put the phone down and walk away.' I'd tried this so many times recently but I could never follow through. I knew it wasn't good for me. That much I'd figured out months ago. Yet I couldn't stop myself. I was addicted but what to exactly, I wasn't sure. 'I've got the willpower of a gnat,' I thought, glancing at the headline. Exam results. 'What now?' I wondered.

Lockdown had taken its toll on every single aspect of life, especially education, but as a private tutor I'd actually found my earnings going up. I was relieved and had to fight with Tom *not* to accept the bank's gracious offer to 'delay' our mortgage payments (I knew they'd only hammer us further down the line). Tom thought it would make life so much easier – no mortgage to worry about for a few months. 'We could save,' he argued. But I knew only too well, we'd blow the lot and regret it later. But even the increase in clients and therefore my income, had its pluses and negatives. In the past few weeks I'd had several irate emails from parents saying their kids were struggling to comprehend even the slightest instruction. 'I just can't seem to get through to her…' was all I seemed to hear. I held my tongue. What I wanted to say was, 'You're only just noticing? I can't get your darling daughter to follow the slightest damned instruction without a fight, why don't you stop spoiling the little brat, doing everything for her, making excuses for her tardiness, trying to control her every waking move, her every waking thought in the name of looking after her and *then* see what happens.'

But I didn't. I didn't say any of that. I needed the money, no matter what I thought of those parents – or their bratty kids.

I took a moment to digest what the article was saying but found I just couldn't concentrate. I was angry just looking at it. Furious in fact. So furious I wanted to throw something but there was nothing but my iPhone to hand and I knew that even if I smashed it, I'd only go out and get myself another and then how would I be any different from the wall breaking buffoon downstairs? Get a hold of yourself Galena, I thought – it's Tom, he's getting to you. You need a break. A trip out to the shops will do you the world of good.

The drive to the supermarket was slightly odd and I was unable to shake off that same weird vibe I'd experienced in the garden just moments earlier. I passed a line of people at the bus stop who all appeared to be arguing, shouting and gesturing to each other in a frenzy. On every corner it seemed, people were strangely animated – had it always been like this, or was I just not paying attention before? Maybe, like Tom and I, these people were sick to the death of each other. Sick of looking at each other, sick of listening to each other, sick, sick, sick. I resisted the urge to switch on the radio. I couldn't take any more news about the virus; the death count, the rules, the ever-changing advice. Instead, I opened the window and felt a strange pounding sensation on the side of my head.

Tesco was packed. I parked the car and rooted around for my mask, hooking it over my ears. It took some time and I had to keep adjusting the straps, as if somehow my ears had shrunk in the night. I began cursing as I tried to get it to stay put and flung it on the floor before taking a deep breath and trying again. When at last I felt sure it was safe, I ventured over to the entrance, promising myself that I would *not* buy an extra-large bar of chocolate to cheer myself up.

At the entrance I hesitated. I shouldn't need a trolley for just one bottle of milk, but I was a little unsure of the rules. Did I have to have a trolley for monitoring purposes? Or was that rule gone now? I searched around for an assistant but when I shouted over, I realised he too was wired up to his iPhone. He didn't even turn around, so I took a chance and went inside without.

Once inside, it suddenly struck me that supermarkets no longer played that awful jazz music that used to accompany my childhood and teenage shopping trips. I'd hated it when I was young – all those brassy instruments taking melodies in strange directions like scribbles on a page. Jazz had always baffled me, especially the modern stuff. I liked a tune that knew where it was going but that stuff? It ducked and dived all over the place, everywhere but where you expected. That said, suddenly I missed it. I looked inside my bag for my phone and thought about playing some tunes on Spotify – anything to alleviate the boredom.

I had one earbud in, poised to play when I heard some strange noises and turned to stare. There was a woman and two children at the front of the queue and they appeared to be shouting at the teller but I couldn't quite make out what they were saying. I moved closer but the sound was still muffled.

'Ey ont ayr ot u ay – Am elng u, kdz ont eed u are a ask,' said the woman. She was pointing at her children and shaking her head.

'Adam, am orrie. A ant erve u. Is i ools.' The teller shrugged her shoulders. She had that look that people have when they know they hold all the power but want to appear helpless. Like a politician, I thought. Something inside me recoiled.

I shook myself, removing the earbud and poking my finger around in my ear. Whatever they were talking about, was really none of my business, but I couldn't stop that burning curiosity – that longing to stare when you sensed the something big was about to happen, like standing at the edge of a beach waiting for the tsunami.

'A ant ee ot u ayng!' said the woman. She flung her arms wide in the air in a gesture of defeat.

My skin began to tingle a little and I froze. I pressed my palms against my forehead, dread creeping up my spine. Wait. What was going on? Was this it? Was I coming down with something? Was *that* what was happening? There had certainly been some very strange side effects to this virus knocking around and no one quite knew exactly what the symptoms actually were – they were vague at the best of times. We'd just grown to accept it was simply a sickness.

One that affected everyone, right across the globe. The world was terribly, terribly sick. I pulled my mask tighter and it was only then it occurred to me that maybe Tom wasn't being an arse at all. Maybe it was me. I couldn't hear properly. What was wrong with me?

I strained my ears. My throat felt unbearably tight. I did my best to fight the panic and moved closer to the queue. Perhaps I was over-reacting but I had to know. I just had to know for certain…

The teller and the woman seemed to really be going at it now and the woman bent forward and slammed her fist down on the counter but she couldn't have done it very hard because all I heard was a soft thud. That said, it was enough to encourage a few more shoppers to jostle forward in an attempt to break it up.

'Ook am n a urry!' said one of them. I watched his face, trying to follow what he was saying but his lips were hidden by his mask. I breathed a sigh of relief, almost laughing at myself. That was it! The masks. There was nothing wrong with my hearing at all and my temperature was just fine. The reason I couldn't hear was because of the masks.

The shop assistant raised her eyes to the ceiling and pressed a buzzer on her counter. A red light lit up at the end of her station.

'Avno lue ot ur ayng. Am ot eelng ell. All et elp.' She slumped down at her counter and rubbed her head.

A store supervisor arrived several minutes later. His face twisted as the teller explained the situation. He kept shaking his head and tugging at his left ear.

'Ot?' he said. Someone else jutted in, but by now all I could hear was a jumble of noises getting louder and louder inside my head. I started to feel nauseous.

'Can I please have some help?' I yelled. 'I don't feel too good.'

A few people turned to look at me but their faces were contorted. I staggered to one side and the crowd jumped back. Someone appeared to speak to me. I gestured to his mask and my ears. 'I'm sorry,' I said, 'I can't understand you, it's the mask.' I pointed to his mouth which seemed to make him even more angry.

Within seconds I was surrounded by people – all huddled round me forming a circle, jumbling up their words. I remembered a game I'd played at primary school where whoever was 'it' had to stand in the middle of a circle blindfolded. They were twisted round and round until the whole world began to spin and were then expected to find their way back to the others while they (inevitably) scarpered. When whoever was 'it' did manage to touch someone, that person had to fall to their knees in defeat.

I tried to glance over their heads, searching for the exit but something must have gone wrong with my eyesight because I couldn't read any of the signs. One by one the other customers started dropping to the floor just like I had, a look of confusion in their eyes as they struggled to make themselves heard.

I reached in my bag, panicked, and grabbed my phone, scrolling up and down the screen, searching for advice, help, anything. My chest clenched like a fist. None of it made any sense, not a word of it. Not a single thing. As I held it, I felt it vibrate and it was only then I realised it was ringing but even the ringing sounded distorted – like a scream. I attempted to answer it, but I couldn't hear with so many people shouting around me.

I curled into a ball and recognised what I thought was Tom's voice coming out of the phone.

'An u et me a oaf o ed? Eve un out.'

I opened my mouth but my head went blank. There was something I was supposed to do, I could feel it in my body – a sensation, a tingling a knowing – like the feeling a bird surely has when it gets ready to migrate for the winter, singing its very last song of summer before it departs.

But for the life of me, I just couldn't tell you what it was.

Murder at Clown School

Lizzie Hudson

'A clown falls so that we don't have to.'
– Unknown

Things happen like this: Sophie wouldn't have met Victor if she hadn't lost her bus pass. The bus pass cost £12.50 for the week, bought and newly printed out every Monday morning. But this week by Tuesday afternoon it must have fallen through the hole in her inside coat pocket. Until her mum gave her money again next Monday, Sophie would have to walk to school forty minutes each morning, through the bright red estate, over the bridge, all along the canal.

That first early October walk, that was when she met him. Victor came to walk next to her and he asked her which school year she was at in. Some point between morning and afternoon that day was when obsession reared its head like a grossly loving Labrador, all in Sophie's very tender imagination.

That was what began the turn of events that ended up in Sophie having to drop out, with no other option but to apply to clown school.

AUDITIONING FOR CLOWN SCHOOL

Getting into clown school was … not easy.

One of the judges was one of the most famous clowns in the world. One of them was a leading academic in studies of theatre and failure. The third was a very renowned director of Hollywood cinema.

The rumours online were that if you choked your clown school audition, they would immediately throw you out. If you fucked up your words or forgot your dance moves there was … no second chance. You could never apply again.

There were even rumours that at clown school some people went for their auditions and never came back to the world after.

Sophie and her friends at clown school still hadn't figured out how or why they passed the rigorous entrance exam and interviews, or what it was they had been looking for.

Here were some of the questions they could remember being asked in the interview:

- Have you ever been in LOVE?
- Have you ever killed anyone?
- Have you ever thought you could kill someone?
- Do you have a good relationship with your family?
- Do you prefer to eat with your fingers or a knife and fork?
- Do you prefer to eat with a knife to a fork?

For a lot of the questions, Sophie answered NO, then crossed it out, then answered YES then was still unsure.

But there is something about the exam – everyone says it – there is something that it changes in you and Sophie and her clown school friends had all felt it when they walked out of the building the moment after the interview. It's as if you forget everything that happened, like you were wiped blank of it, like a spell.

Maybe this is the reason that they all got into clown school; this unfathomable, unifying factor. Maybe this is the reason they were all so scared to leave.

Sophie was one of the only girls at clown school.

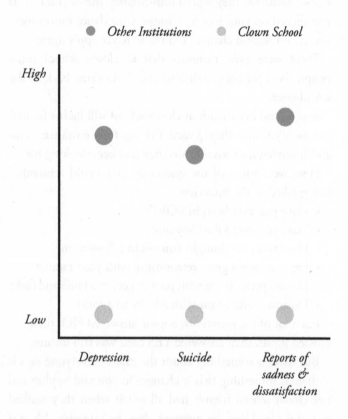

'Don't be worried,' the boys and men at clown school would say. 'We are feminists. You're safe with us.'

And they'd hug her from behind when she wasn't expecting and grab at her very soft armpits and it made her scream.

And that was before anyone was allowed so much as a lick of face paint.

Before Clown School Sophie was just like other boys, girls, etc.

Sophie put her hair in a ponytail. Sophie was okay at maths and okay at English. Sophie ate paninis in the old school canteen and had a phone that was called a Blackberry which she went on when she was sat with her friends at lunch time. (This was later handed in, of course, when she first arrived at clown school, locked away in a cupboard and never seen again by Sophie.)

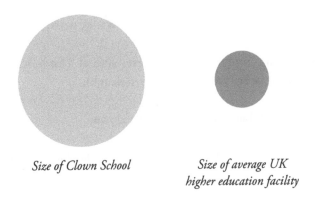

Size of Clown School

*Size of average UK
higher education facility*

Everything changed when Sophie met Victor. Within a week Sophie felt like she had thrown up her soul out of her own actual mouth and the only way she could get it back would be if Victor were to make her his girlfriend.

Victor was a normal boy and very much a real boy. He only seemed to have three jumpers. The brown one, the blue one, the grey one. Sophie longed to put her hands in their pockets or wear one of them as if she did not have one of her own, stretch their wide cuffs around her hands to make her look small.

Loving Victor – even the hope of a dramatic love confession and eventually being with Victor – was impossible. But for Sophie this was this great pathos, a place for Sophie to redirect all of the desire and longing she had held in her tiny heart for almost eighteen years.

Sophie didn't know this herself though she was intelligent enough to have figured it out: Victor could have been anyone. All Sophie could think of was him.

That was the reason Sophie lost her mind. Without it, she would never have ended up at clown school.

GRADUATING FROM CLOWN SCHOOL

Something Sophie kept from everyone at clown school (not even in her bedsheets not even drunk).

Sophie…

Sophie did not even want to be a clown.

Sophie thought that this was just her.

But really most of the students at clown school feel like this.

A VISITOR AT CLOWN SCHOOL

An announcement was made one Monday that Gustav du Sang, the most famous clown of all, was coming to visit the students at clown school.

Gustav du Sang used to be part of a famous touring duo, The Two Birds, with his wife, Anastacia, until she died one afternoon in a hot air balloon accident. Du Sang himself had been the only other passenger aboard the hot air balloon. It was so traumatic for him that any of the information around her death had completely disappeared from his memory when interviewed by the police.

Ever since then, he had not been able to perform but made his living travelling around giving talks and teaching.

He was very large and very charming.

The headmaster of clown school announced in the assembly that during du Sang's residency he was going to take one student to mentor, to be his protegee.

Could it be Sophie?

Of course not.

Everyone at clown school was preparing for their auditions. Sophie's friends were sewing their costumes and balancing on large red plastic balls and watching their faces in the mirror. They were ordering quantities of white birds and bright insects on Amazon, strips of cloth that look like fires and oceans, shrinking powder, fake guns.

Sophie was more just fixated on watching du Sang all of the time. She noticed what he ate and which of the tutors he sat with and where he seemed to like to walk around. Sometimes he would sit and observe some of the classes or stop groups of students in the corridor to ask them a couple of questions.

For Sophie's audition she dressed up in white. Her plan was to perform a complicated stunt in which she danced against a black background, then she would disappear like smoke into a big paper cloud that was behind her.

But when the time came to perform the trick Sophie choked. She just stood on the stage and cried, crying too hard to even move. Her white face-paint was running all disgusting down her face.

And that's when du Sang stood up and started slowly applauding and applauding. He said, 'This is the best piece of theatre I've seen all day. You are the biggest clown in all of clown school.'

When the time came for the assembly in which du Sang's protege was announced it came as a surprise to everyone.

The protegee was Sophie.

Over the coming weeks he took Sophie for meetings in his makeshift office (that's the back of his car.)

He bounced with her on trampolines, told her of his history. One time he grabbed her by the shoulders and shook her until she felt sick. It was an exercise. He dressed her up as different types of animals: a squirrel, a big bird, a rabbit, various bugs.

She is meant for learning, he tells her, it is like she was born to be taught.

Sophie felt finally confirmed of something she had always known but a few times recently, occasionally, she had begun to doubt

but it turned out it was true:

it is that she had always been the special one, the best one, the golden girl, there is a talent she had that even should she cease to use it would always shine through.

Sophie began to understand why it was that du Sang knew to select her. Even though she barely spoke in front of him and even though in a way she was very terrified of him, she understood, as du Sang kept telling her, that there was a very profound connection between them. It is like what she felt with Victor but in another form, a greater, purer form, for what had Sophie ever wanted more than to be taught, to be finally given the answers she needed about what to wear, how to act, how to think.

This is why what happened next came as such a shock to Sophie

because he took her into his office

and made her miss a performance

and made her miss dinner
and he told her
that she had to leave clown school.

Before this Sophie had rarely ever asked him anything or questioned his judgement. But when he told her to leave clown school she said why why why and she screamed and cried and begged him not to ask her to do that (for she would have died rather than disobey him).

'I belong in clown school. Clown school is the only place I have ever been, and all the other places were not really places but roads and moments in a past that led to the present and the present is what is supposed to be happening now, me, in clown school.'

He told her she must be depressed and he has been through much worse so he could understand it twice over.

'You will do much better,' he says, 'out in the real world.'

Sophie started to pack her bags. She was so sad that she could not speak. She did not tell anyone she was leaving, although people in the dormitories and in her classes mostly knew. When she woke up in those final days she wished she was asleep again. Even though it wasn't compulsory, she kept on attending classes, mostly just not to be alone. She was a walking bag of shame. There was nothing for her.

MURDER AT CLOWN SCHOOL

But one night that week at clown school, a girl went missing.

Clown school was surrounded by a dark wooded area.

The police think that the girl went into the wooded area and died.

Probably there was a man.

They were all sat in dream diary class when they found out

about the missing girl. Sophie was talking about the flowers that grow out of her mouth again. It was a recurring dream.

'Dispel it,' the teacher was saying. 'Spit.'

Sophie spat. Then the deputy head of clown school came into the room and told everyone that Amelia went missing last night after telling her friends she was going for a walk with someone and would not say who.

Everyone in the class was gasping and screaming.

No one was listening to Sophie anymore.

In the coming weeks barely anyone spoke to her or to each other, just at each other, about Amelia. Everyone was constantly crying or holding each other or going over all of the rumours and their theories.

When once she would have been jealous of Amelia, for being the girl that might have been murdered, Sophie was beginning to realise that there was going to be nothing to worry about.

Because everyone seemed to have forgotten that Sophie was supposed to be leaving clown school.

And as for du Sang, he drove away in his car the night of Amelia's disappearance.

Much like when she first came to clown school, Sophie keeps her head down mostly. She sits at the back of the classes and she does not raise her hand to answer questions. She does not answer any questions at all.

Artefacts

Jennifer Isherwood

Normally these sorts of letters are about his Mum. It's been a few months since the last wrangle and the postman's been on time for once, so that's something. Brian takes the official-looking envelope into the kitchen and sets it down on the counter. Twenty-five Castleton Road. There's no hurry to open it. He's used to throwing forms or money at what's left of her problems. All in good time.

First, he clunks the mechanical arm of his espresso machine and spoons fine earthy grounds into the basket he cleaned out, as always, after yesterday morning's coffee. He's not the type to leave muck in his kitchen overnight. He wipes spillage off the marble worktop and sets the machine trickling. The emerging smell welcomes him into the world and makes him feel that a day's work will be possible after all. The daily cup is so small and yet so full of promises: today you will move forward, achieve things, be productive! Feeling under the flap of the envelope, he turns his attention to the garden, which is tinged with morning purple. He surveys the wooden chairs tilted against the solid patio table. The lawn is well-mown. The flowerbeds are dug over, ready for planting in spring. He notes the raggedy rhododendron bushes looming in front of the back fence. They'll need sorting out soon. But, with any luck, the previous year's battles with moss and bindweed will turn out to have been won.

The letter is written on a good quality weight of paper

and announces its authority with a municipal letterhead. It's not one Brian recognises, so he pauses. Then, little hands start wringing out his intestines as he absorbs the information:

Dear Sir or Madam,

I am writing to you on behalf of the Coal Authority, a government organisation that works to protect the public and the environment in coal mining areas.

Seven million properties lie within Britain's coalfields and we have records of over 170 thousand old coal mine shafts. We are now carrying out an inspection programme of those mine shafts as part of our public safety strategy.

Our records show that your house is close to the recorded position of an old mine shaft and we would like to inspect it. Problems with mine shafts are very rare, but it is entirely possible that the foundations of your house, home, sense of self, security and hopes for the future could all implode with astonishing speed and very little notice.

I write this not to alarm you, but to make you aware that everything you have worked for, achieved and acquired is in jeopardy.

Brian knows he'll hit rush hour if he doesn't leave soon, but he can't resist bringing up the Coal Authority website. He soon finds what he's searching for: a rich stream of worst-case scenarios. *Collapse of shallow mine workings ... subsidence ... risk of entry into shafts and adits ... gas emissions...* What would a disused shaft do to the house price? Surely his grandparents would've got the full survey done before they bought the place? The screen bathes his face in blue light while he burrows through windows, forums and threads. Clicking on links, he fizzes each time a new page loads, the time bar always creeping forward just that little bit too slowly: *Spontaneous combustion of coal ... underground heatings ... carbon monoxide ... ground fractures...* And was he going to be compensated if something was really wrong? Or would his case just get buried somewhere under a pile of solicitors' letters? Like Grandpa's.

The letter slips onto the floor as he throws the coffee down his throat and heads for the back door. The cranky lock frustrates his fingers. Why has he still not got that fixed, for pity's sake? The more he tries, the harder it seems to find the right combination of twist and pressure. It's impossible. He's trapped in his own bloody kitchen! Still wrestling with the key, he lifts his foot to kick the door and then the lock turns – easy as that – as if the whole thing was just a joke to get a rise out of him. The neighbourhood is still quiet but he advances across the patio like a man squaring up to a boozy high street. Cold air crunches into his chest.

The perfect lawn winks at him.

Clunking sounds? Muffled voices? He turns and there's no one there. The rhododendrons rustle. Or is that the sweep of broom?

He crouches to get closer to the ground and lowers himself onto hands and knees. Underneath, something shifts, like those tussocks up on the moors that wobble when you put a boot on one. His hands test the ground, searching for whatever it was that just gave way, but everything just feels cold and hard again, unwilling to open up. He doesn't notice the dirt grinding itself into his dry-cleaned white shirt as he leans down further and presses his cheek to the grass, listening.

'Hello? Is someone down there?'

Then he feels a jolt in his elbow and up through his shoulders, as if the ground has moved again. But still the surface feels solid. Wriggling his fingers, Brian finds a piece of turf to grip onto and manages to yank away a small strip. It's not easy but he gets a bit of purchase on another chunk. After gouging out that piece he finds a rhythm and is soon pulling up handfuls of earth. Ignoring tremors in his knees, he bends to his work, as though deep down he is still his younger self on the beach at Filey, burrowing with all his heart for Australia. Hot breaths push out of his lungs. Is that a shaft of light from deep underground? He keeps digging, further and further, until a crack appears and the beam of a head torch glamours his eyes. He blinks furiously, trying to keep sight lines open, and then –

'Grandma?'

Brian's pupils have shrunk to needle points but they still can't keep out enough light.

'Oh yes. I'm glad you popped by. Your grandpa and I were just talking about you.'

'Grandpa's down there too?'

'Yes love. Just his normal self. Well, normal for now anyway.' A wheezy chuckle echoes around, as if through caverns. 'So d'you want to come down and help me with this puzzle? Only I think I've gone and lost a corner piece down in a crevice somewhere. And you'll be wanting tea, won't you? We don't have that fancy coffee of yours.'

'Phyllis!'

'Alright dear! I'm just talking to our Brian.'

He hears a wrenching, guttural sound.

'Grandpa?'

'Brian is it? Let's have a look at you then.'

Brian peers down, trying to make out shapes and movement, but the light is making everything else around it darker.

'That's no good. Straighten yourself up lad. You're better than this.'

'You think?'

'Arthur! Don't mind him Brian. He's not well and he doesn't much like it above-ground these days.'

Somewhere in the darkness, Brian brushes against the vague grey shape of his Mum, sitting rigid among her pills on the settee while his grandma and grandpa arrived with road maps and picnic paraphernalia, chivvying Brian to find his anorak. Mum would flinch when they flung back the curtains. Brian didn't remember her ever waving goodbye at the door.

Someone's got to give the poor lad a chance!

His grandparents made a point of taking him off to historical sights: Hadrian's Wall, Holy Island, York Minster. On these trips, he forgot about home and he discovered that you found history by digging. Artefacts. He'd learned that word from his grandpa. He'd had to learn a new word every trip and practise times tables in the car before the bag of sweets came out. Artefacts. Cold hard facts in the ground.

Brian had taken his son, Jamie, to York Minster not long after grandpa's funeral. There was an exhibition on about the excavation of the Crypt, about the different layers the archaeologists had found there: Medieval, Norman, Saxon, Roman. People leaving their marks, making the place important. Jamie had been running down the stone passage-ways and making echoing spat spat spat sounds with his feet. It had stung Brian to suspect that his son was bored. An afternoon in front of the flat screen would probably have worked better. Brian could never find his grandpa's way of making the past seem urgent or interesting. Now, with his face pressed against the damp earth of his back lawn, Brian remembers how he'd stood still in the belly of the Minster, feeling the future pushing down on him and the past rising up from below. Jamie scampering away from him, a resurfacing childhood wish that his mum could have been there. Brian had felt something in the damp dark of that place but couldn't find the words to give to Jamie. He'd checked his watch. Time running away with itself again. The lad needed to be dropped off back with Julie in an hour and a half.

Come on Jamie, let's go and get you some pop and crisps for the drive home.

Jamie had perked up, Brian remembered, as the car had propelled them through the Vale of York, round Leeds, and down onto the M1 back to Sheffield. He'd flicked the child lock off so Jamie could get out before walking him across the concrete. Then he'd waited at the base of the dark stairwell, listening to his son's footsteps clanging, until a light cracked at the door of Julie's flat. That light had shone in his eyes all the way home.

Coming home after that day, twenty-five Castleton Road had felt like an empty shell. After this morning's letter, it's now bursting at the seams, crammed full of life savings, trophy purchases, and plans for the future. Something to pass onto Jamie, even if he couldn't live there now. Brian finds himself scrunching the hard earth with his hands. This is his land, his little piece of being taken seriously. He remembers the first time he stood in the garden, not as a visiting grandson but as a home-owner: someone who had finally grown up and taken a chunk out of the adult world. 'An Englishman's home is his Castleton Road!' his grandpa used to say, when he still had enough puff to chase Brian round his garden, clattering with broomstick guns behind deck chair barricades. Back then, who could have known how it would all end up? That Grandpa would be left defending his keep against the besieging bank, waiting for his compensation money, and no one else finding out until it was nearly too late.

Dirt presses into the tender skin beneath Brian's finger-nails and he closes his eyes to savour the pain. He's fought for this house too.

There was that awful row at the funeral, when it all came out. No, Grandma didn't know if the pay-out was due, and no, it might not be enough to save the house. And that's right, his mum never cared so long as the handouts kept coming. Brian remembers grabbing a pork pie from the buffet table and then storming out towards the rainy carpark.

You've all been burying your heads in the sand!

A few weeks later, Grandma had accepted Brian's money quietly.

A knight in a fancy suit with a trusty cheque book. That was what his mum called him at the time. He tries to see her now, turning back in the doorway of twenty-five Castleton Road one last time, but the light is behind her and he can't make out her features. How she would cackle if she knew the house was crumbling from under him. But this morning, with the damp bleeding into his clothes and a taste of soil in his mouth, he sees his offer for what it was, as she must have seen it then: a land grab.

Of course, he'd seen that Julie and her lawyers never got their hands on the place either. But at what cost? Brian feels cracks everywhere, forming and transforming themselves with every inward and outward breath. It was what Grandma and Grandpa wanted, he tells himself again. Was it though? He can barely bring himself to ask, but something is erupting:

'Alone for the first time in forty-three years. I was never going to last long without your grandpa. In that house on my own, I understood more about your mum, I think. Spending all that money she didn't have. How maybe she couldn't help herself. But Arthur and me, we'd already talked about it and, if we could, we wanted to leave something for you to build on. A garden for Jamie to play in. Somewhere for your mum to come back and stay if she needed to.'

'Aye and there's been so much building. To think of all that money pouring in round here. You've done well for yourself, lad. You haven't got left behind.'

'But what should I do now?'

There is nothing.

'Grandpa?'

Brian listens, but there are no more voices and he is alone. Light sinks down onto him, onto everything: the flowerbeds, the garden furniture, the big fence, a deflated red football of Jamie's nestling under the rhododendron bush.

And then he is suddenly very small, crouching in a tiny ball of space inside that same bush, right by the trunk. His bare legs are being stroked by the waxy leaves and he is enjoying the mulchy perfume of the flowers, which are just turning brown at the edges. He has been hiding out for weeks he thinks.

Now there are hands exploring a gap in the leaves, fingers with chipped purple nail varnish, followed by the face of his mother, red and puffy but unlined. She was so very young. It becomes clear to him how the corners of her green eyes and her mouth turned naturally downwards, sloping off the sides of her face. It was as if smiling for her entailed a fight against the forces of gravity. But the face appearing through the rhododendron leaves is lifting itself into a grin.

'Found you!'

He listens for more, lying on his back now, palms flat against the dewy grass. Harder and harder he listens – searching splotches of memory for a bedroom, a face, a feeling – but there is nothing certain. He is being called away by the sounds of children shouting as they head for the school bus, by the hum of cars pulling out of driveways, their stereos pulsing with breakfast radio beats. A curtain is being drawn back. All down the street, houses are giving up their occupiers to the working world, which gathers them in. He sits up and then goes back inside. The coffee grounds need cleaning out, and there are many other things to be done.

Ramona's Square

Dan Robinson

This is the master bedroom, in the corner of the four-bed dormer bungalow. Great views. A big lawn. To the east, open fields and sky. To the north, shadows of a majestic Cedar of Lebanon reach towards the wood. She is sitting up in bed. He's not there. She lifts a glass of water to her mouth. Mint backwash. She sets the glass down and breathes in, seeking the ache in her lower back. The weight of her head finds the new pillow. The ceiling paper has a repeat pattern that can't quite be fathomed. The red digits of the LED clock are reflected back in the window. 06:22. It's Tuesday. She has three days' annual leave left and this is her last chance to use it or lose it. She's been dreaming. A spoon on her tongue. Long thin fingers bent at right-angles. The legs of a cricket or king prawn. Something like gristle.

She slides her legs out and pads to the side table. A faux-Edwardian piece with mirrored drawer fronts and brass drop handles. She takes her hairbrush and lifts the laptop lid.

Scanning up and down, flitting left and right. A jump, a jolt.

She leans in. The screen casts light on her forehead. Something else is here. Things moving. Shapes seen from above. It's like research. It's like a game. In the half-light of her bedroom. It's like a dance.

She's in statistics. Algorithms and predictions. It's all shapes. This project is a helix, that one a square. The systems behind it all. Her husband is different. He sells furniture and interiors. He likes immediacy. Holding an object in his hand and feeling its weight. To be busy with people. An eye for colour. He'll stop in the street and point at the light on a car door or someone's coat. He's salesman of the month for Alberto's Boutique and can make three grand in a good week. Right now, he's at some expat's lime-rendered château in Menton, France. She could have gone with him but no. A plane is overhead and a dog is barking outside. She would never have chosen this table, nor these curtains. He got them back after a photoshoot. The green curtains are thick velvet, floor to ceiling. They did look good in the magazine. A second monitor linked to her laptop holds a grainy moving image.

A blurry dot flies across.

Must be a bird getting food or something for a nest. The black and white image in high contrast has texture. It was his idea, the surveillance tower, the drones. But she's the one who attends to it. Until contracts are exchanged anything can happen. 'The lengths some people will go to,' he'd said. 'We didn't spend precious time with architects and surveyors just to see it all go to shit,' he'd said. The surveillance was only meant to be a few weeks but ten months later she's still waking up to aerial views and the changing seasons of the field. Sketchy patches of first snow had reminded her of the painting by Piero de la Francesca on a poster at her aunt's. Angels with lutes. A naked baby Jesus on a blue cloth in a landscape of – snow? She looked more closely on her next visit: *The Nativity, 1470–75*. There's no snow. It did seem there was, or should be. Months later, waves of hay rippled across the screen in the august heat. Wimbledon was no competition.

She picks the mustard cashmere from the wardrobe and her beige comfy trousers. She lays them out on the bed. She's just been away with him. A weekend in Braemar, Scotland. A quiet meander and words by the boulder, a glacial erratic. Wind on her ears. She needed these moments away. His postcard is propped up to the side of the laptop screen.

The field of hay from above. Figures walk towards the tractor.

She leans forward. Which boy is which? Why aren't they ever in school?

The first morning in Braemar had been cold and bright. Seven degrees at 11:00 am. Scrambling over the basalt, some distance between them, then through the heather with pink-orange sun on their faces. Fighting the developers had been a strain but here they are. He's more accustomed to wrangling. It saps her energy. Calculations, degrees of uncertainty, what-ifs. It's not even over yet. It was good being away. When he grazed his arm on a thorn – a long red line – she measured it with her outstretched hand like an octave on a piano. She pictures the Scottish trip as an interlocking mass. The orangey light. The weight of his gait – sixty-five kilos. Some sort of conversation about happiness and sadness. She'd laughed when he hung his arm dramatically over the side of the bath like that other painting – *The Death of Marat*. In bed she'd pushed against his jaw with the heel of her hand. An even distribution of weight. A balance of pressure and enquiry. Yes. It was good. The postcard is a reminder. Or a confirmation. She picks it up and turns it over. He wrote it at the breakfast table and posted it home. The printed type reads, 'An early summer display of wild rhododendrons by the loch side looking south-east to the hills of Braemar forest.' His handwriting is large and slanted. She leans the card back against the lamp.

At the right-hand side of the screen the bright white square starts to move, up.

She pulls her padded stool closer.

The tractor will cut the field of hay from the outside in. The first full circuit follows the boundary fence. Then it's ever decreasing squares. This is how it is. A rhythm builds. Each straight is shorter than the last, the turns more frequent. Turn left. And left. Who's driving? Could be either of them, fourteen and sixteen. Anticlockwise. Winding in. A game of her own making. The field opposite her house. The lads in the tractor. Camera one, thirty-eight feet high on a galvanised tower. She switches to the trackpad. Camera two. She straightens her back on the stool and watches the screen. What time is it? 9:15 am.

When they reach the centre, the two dots dismount the tractor. Surely the older one had been driving? The tractor had done tight turns, in on itself. Left. Left again. Like a computer game. Like *Pac-Man*. Now the hay has shrunk to a patch. This is what they do. Leave a bit, just enough. Her thumb and fingers open out against the touchscreen laptop. Zoom in. She presses a key. Outside the house and across the road, the black drone hovers, silent like a falcon threaded to a cloud. The lens rotates. She waits. The tractor is still, the engine quiet. A trace of the concentric squares can be seen. The tractor roof in the blinding sun is a brilliant white square. Zoom further in. The boy-blobs mess about on the cut hay. Each on their own pinched shadow. One pulls the other by the jacket.

Her curtains are still drawn. Her bed has been made with care: the silk sheet straightened out, the throw nicely aligned, gold tassels top-to-bottom, not side-to-side.

Only the small square of uncut grass remains. The lads stand by. Things are moving inside the square. Small shapes moving. The boys are quite still now. She counts seven rabbits in the square of hay. The patch must be two meters across. Fuzzy rabbits in a huddle. They'll make a run for it. It's a waiting game. The lads hold their jackets ready like nets.

Off they go. One lad throws his jacket and gets two at once. Her eyes widen. Sit on them. She zooms back out and pans right with the trackpad. It's now. He holds one between the knees, the other must be warm in his hand, the fur smooth. A quick chop to the back of the neck. He's holding its feet. Bash on the ground. Again. The body must be limp.

She'd like to be up close to it. The smell of the field. Hay on her shoes.

She walks across the carpet in her socks to the top of the staircase. Through the small window on the stairs there is a dark lumpen shrub, at the front of the house. A laurel. The top is bobbing about, its leaves shimmering behind the glass. Over the years it has edged outward, and she has pruned it back. The glossy leaves are dark. There is a space beneath, big enough to lay sheltered. Where a child might hide.

Leaves have fallen on the white angular gravel where the weeds come up. Her aunt says the house looks like a seventies golf lodge. From the bottom step she crosses the kitchen and pulls the cord to open the blind. Over the road the field is bright with grasses, seed heads and young saplings.

The boys are coming.

She opens the kitchen drawer and gets the money from the tin. Wires connect her house to a telegraph pole across the road. This in turn connects to further poles running the full length of the A627. If she were to call the house opposite, a signal would travel some distance to a switchboard or exchange. A text message would bounce off a satellite. There is no need for a conversation with their mother.

She opens the front door. Dry leaves scratch on the path. They each look the same but different. They're in jeans, pale T-shirts and white socks. Two younger versions of a man. They don't say anything. What would they say? The younger one has his jacket open with both hands in his pockets and his mouth open. The older one has the two rabbits in his hand. He hands them to her and with her other hand she gives them each a five-pound note. All in one movement.

'Thanks,' she says.

They all stand there for a moment. Long enough for thoughts.

She closes the door. For a few more seconds both of them look at her through the rippled glass, their silhouettes all broken in jagged lines. They turn and run off over the road, getting smaller. She moves to the window and lays the rabbits on the metal drainer by the sink. She likes to stand here and look out.

She'll go down soon and hang them in the cellar.

Everywhere's in the
Middle of Everywhere

Richard Smyth

When I look at them I can feel the humming in my ears. Feel it, not hear it. It rattles the little bones that live in my ears. Eggborough, Ferrybridge, and Drax. Holy things come in threes.

There was a young lad by the pond the other day, fishing. I say shouldn't you be in school. He says he's on climate strike. I say pull the other one lad, and he says no, for real, climate strike, it's legit, look at that Greta Thunberg, has every Friday off, and I say I don't know who that is but I bet you you don't see her stood by Middleton Park pond with a fishing rod and a tupperware full of maggots. He says fuck off.

So it must have been a Friday. You lose track.

From up here at the top of the old golf course you can see all three and on clear days you can see even further. Not as far as the sea I don't think but who knows really. You can see the sun, can't you, and that's a good way off. I mean a good way off. I'm not sure what's beyond the sea exactly. What if I started walking and just didn't stop? What if I just swam across the sea like it was nothing more than that fishpond and walked up the beach at the other side and then just walked and walked. Where would I get to? Persia or one of those places. India? I don't know.

The thing is though that it's easy enough to walk and

walk and not get anywhere at all. Walking's easy, it's walking straight that's the trick. I can't tell you much but I can tell you that.

Dog chased a squirrel in here seventeen year ago and here I still am. Dog's long gone but I'm still here.

Found a stick earlier, a good one, three foot long, beech I think, nice bit of knobble at the heavy end. Had to chase off a feller who was at the mushrooms. They grow along the old fairway, in the old rough, dozens of them at this time of year. I know they're not mine exactly but they weren't his either. Lad with a curly moustache and a satchel. Said he was foraging. I said forage somewhere else. Forage in Morley or Carlton, I cried, as I chased him down the fairway. Forage in Tingley or Rothwell or Ouzlewell Green, forage in Churwell or Flushdyke or Gomersall or Gildersome, forage in Methley or Kippax or Allerton Bywater.

I ran out of breath before I ran out of places for him to forage. Anyway he was out of sight before I got to Kippax. Quick as a squirrel.

Don't forage fucking here, I shouted. Don't forage in fucking Middleton.

Middle of where? Middle of nowhere. Middle of everywhere. Everywhere's the middle of everywhere, really.

The thing about mushrooms is they're fine, they're all fine, you mustn't listen to those who say oh they're poisonous, oh they'll kill you, they won't kill you, they're fine. The worst they'll do is give you a dizzy spell or a few days of the runs. The thing to remember is that hardly anything kills you. I can't tell you much but I can tell you that. Look at me. Still here.

The sky rolls over and over, white as a sheep, boil-washed, and the energy of the world rushes upwards into the tall bodies of the trees. You can't stand where I'm standing, here on this dirty grass, among these screaming birds, and tell me you don't feel it too.

I wake up from a dream with my face half-buried in leaf-mould.

I remember, after a while, why I fell asleep like that. In that part of the woods is where the coal miners used to hew (a funny, whistling word, that – hew!). I remember pressing my cheek into the mulchy earth to listen for the coal miners down there below. Of course they're not there in person. I suppose their old bones might be, some of them. But do you know, astro-scientists tell us that, somewhere in the universe, we can still listen to the echoes of the noise made by the very beginning of everything. The very beginning of everything. And of course that was a good long time ago. So I lay down to listen to the echoes of the miners: their talking, shouting, banging, clattering, weeping, singing (surely they sang, everyone sings).

I don't remember hearing anything.

Then a bit later, while I'm walking with my stick across what I think was once the fourteenth hole, I remember the dream.

I'm up at the top of the fairway again, but I'm not by myself, not like usual. There's a bunch of people, mostly men, some women, all in smart dark suits. They're listening to me. I'm telling them things and they're listening.

What I'm talking about is energy, power.

Do you mean, they say, the energy of Eggborough, Drax, Ferrybridge, because yes, it's as you say, we can feel it – we can feel it in our earbones (anvil, hammer, stirrup: holy things come in threes, it's as you say).

My voice is big when I say no, no, and (with a sweeping arm gesture) say that I mean this energy, the energy of this wild place – this crucible of life, east of the Dewsbury Road, north of the A653. And by that – I know this in the dream – I mean the uprushing of the blades of grass, the hydraulics of the trees, the untiring bellows of breath and birdsong, the uncheckable momentum of the seasons, the clenched potentiality of rock and earth and clay and coal, the strength of flowers, the perpetual motion of midges.

Let Ferrybridge run to dereliction and be overrun by deer and rosebay, I cry. Let roosting starlings blacken the walls of Drax. Let Eggborough lie dead and cold, let the grass grow over. Let us no longer hew (I whistle the word like a lapwing) and burn. Let us tap instead the energy of life, gentlemen, ladies, of life.

They are all silent, the people in dark smart suits. They nod, with slack jaws.

All except one, a man, whose suit seems not quite as smart as the suits of the others. In the silence he says, this is not correct, Mr (he calls me by a name I forgot a good long while ago). This energy, this power of wild things. Let us consider it, he says (does he draw out a notebook, a ledger of accounts, a spreadsheet?). The labour of the squirrels, let us say – the hard work of this or that caterpillar, the toil of the growing hazel. What is it?

The question seems what's the word, rhetorical, and I don't answer.

It is not surplus, he says. It is used, it is spent, it is needed. Every ounce, every inch. All at once the man, in the dream, seems to be standing very close to me. It's apparent all of a sudden that this is an important man, more important than the rest (are the rest even still there?)

Look at you, Mr (that name again, like a swear word). Consider yourself as a wild thing. Do you, sir, have energy to give away? Look at you. Can you spare a bone, can you spare a breath?

In the dream I consider myself as a wild thing, a life composed of unlikely odds, a creature of extremity, all edge, all twitch, and I say (fearfully, I think) – no, no. And the man makes a mark in his book. The others – they are still there, then – have already turned away from me, and talk among themselves.

I think of the dream again when in the middle of the night I wake up half-curled in my form beneath the holly, shivering hard beneath the conversations of the owls, and again I think – in fact I think I might say it out loud – no, I can't, I can't spare a breath, sir, not a bone, not an ounce, not an inch.

I look down at the city in the aching blue dawn. The tall buildings like big teeth. Chimneys trailing steam, pink in the sunrise. It's so small. I can't look at a city and not think that. Look how little, how low. All those years and all that work and all those people and look – how we barely reach a finger's width into the sky, how we've barely raised ourselves off our elbows. You can lift up your thumb, held sideways, and blot it all out. I do that now. Gone. Nothing. Just one westward rising drift of steam.

I collect some mushrooms. I pick some berries. I find a dead magpie, not too far gone. I lay some traps (my traps are shit, and never work). I gather fistfuls of what leaves are left. I fish the body of a dead cat from the pond – it has a collar, a name, George, and I bury it beneath waxy beech leaves up by the mines.

I lie on my back on the cold soil and watch woodpigeons and aeroplanes crisscross the sky.

I wonder if I'll be here forever. What's forever?

It'll be okay in the end, they say – they say, cleverly, if it's not okay, it's not the end. Well if I'm not still here maybe it's not forever. Does that make sense? My mouth is dry from the mushrooms.

To keep going is the thing. Whether you wind up in Persia or India or under a holly bush in LS-ten or wherever. Keep going. There's an old collier's train down the arse end of the park, a hundred-odd years old – that's still going. No coal to carry but it's still going. Never mind the why, there isn't a why. The trees, they're even older than that, half of them. The world: the world's a good age, a good age. Still spinning. Still going.

Beside the old cart track in the woods I set the sole of my boot against the trunk of a fallen tree and roll it over onto its back – peer at its wet belly. Woodlice all across the pulpy bark.

They remind me –

They remind me that I have other dreams, dreams that feel more like memories than dreams. It's not quite gone, all that (nothing's ever quite gone, is it – ask the leafmould, the clay, the rock, the atoms of the air).

An industrial unit, not far from here, lined with humming mesh cages, where they breed soldier flies for food (fishfood, pigfood, dogfood, until the licensing laws change, and then just food) – was I there, did I do that, raising the young maggots on bakery waste and coffee grounds, drawing up tabulations of carbon outflow and protein content?

Or a factory floor in a salt-washed town beyond the power stations where the air's a reek of fish and bunker fuel – was I there, was I a builder (a menial, probably, a worker ant) of the great encrusted marine turbines that catch this wind, this same cold old Middleton wind, and ratchet it tight into the earth, into batteries, copper cables, capacitors, I don't know what?

Did I nurse young hazel saplings, tubed in clear Perspex, hundreds of them, hundreds of thousands of them, green-timbered and limber and bending their backs in the easterlies, to be chipped for biofuel, did I clear the open meadows in the east (they were bad pasture, anyway) and dig in footings for the solar arrays?

I don't know what I did. They seem like more than dreams though, don't they. I watch the woodlice. I wouldn't want to eat them myself and that's saying something.

If they're dreams, these, they're dreams about persistence. About keeping on. Maybe everything's gone but that. Not just for me but for everyone – everyone down there in that city I just blotted out with my grubby thumb, everyone way over there in Persia or India or wherever it was, and everyone in between – everyone everywhere, we're just keeping going, never mind what for, where to, good or bad, it's just that, keep going.

People talk about 'keeping the lights on' but I think if the lights went off we'd all just keep on walking in the dark.

On days like today when I stand in the ankle-high grass and reach down through myself to feel whatever it is that's coming up through the roots and the fungus – on days like today, I feel like one of those polythene men you used to see on car-dealer forecourts, those ones with the compressed air rushing through them, making them stand upright, wave their arms, dance, bend, beckon. That's me. Without the energy I find here I'd just collapse to the ground, a heap of dirty clothes, an empty bag of skin and hair.

Who knows, maybe it works the other way too. Maybe if I wasn't here the whole place would just go spiralling downwards into nowhere like water out of a bath.

Another reason to keep going. I'd hate to see that happen.

In the dusk of whatever day it is today I stand at the top of the fairway and squint across at the distant lights of the power stations. Feel again the thrum, the tremor – wherever the bloody hell it comes from.

I think about lying down once again and pressing my ear to the wet earth and listening once again for the old songs of the mining men. I don't, yet. I will eventually. But for now I stay standing up and looking over at the lights, because as long as I'm still standing up I'm still standing up. I can't tell you much but I can tell you that. As long as I'm still going I'm still going.

Not Cricket

William Thirsk-Gaskill

The first thing Daniel and I decide is where the last test will be held: where the series is going to finish. We agree that it will be at The Home Of Cricket, Headingley. Headingley is on the drive at seventeen Chelwood Avenue, Moortown, Leeds. Daniel and I have just finished our first year at high school. For the first test, the drive will be Edgbaston, and then Trent Bridge, the Oval, Lords, and finally, Headingley: a five-test series, 200 wickets to fall, unless there are any declarations. Declarations in this era of cricket are rare, unless I have to go home early.

Pauline, Daniel's mum, comes out with a basket of washing to be hung on the line in the back garden. On her way back with the empty basket, she pauses to listen to our discussions about cricket venues. She goes back through the side door of the house, smiling and shaking her head. She leaves the door open. Behind Daniel's shoulder, I get a glimpse of Alex, known as 'Laggy' (Alex's best attempt so far at pronouncing his own name). Alex stares at me, and then disappears. Alex has bright ginger hair, like Alan, Pauline's second husband. I can hear Pauline shouting 'LUCIAN! LUCIAN! WHEN ARE YOU GETTING UP?' Lucian is Daniel's oldest sibling. He is four years older than Daniel and me. He does boxing and weightlifting, and is taking drama classes. He won his first three weightlifting competitions, but did unexpectedly badly in the last one, after which he wrote 'I WILL RETURN' with a black, felt-tip pen on the wall of the bedroom he shares with Daniel.

Daniel tosses the coin. I call 'heads'. Heads it is. I decide to bat.

'Who have your selectors chosen to open the batting with?' asks Daniel.

'Brearley and Boycott.' Daniel nods.

Daniel puts a piece of a broken brick on the drive to mark the start of his run-up. He is captain of his school football team, and plays for the cricket team as an all-rounder. He has been asked to play rugby union and rugby league but turned down the requests, to concentrate on football and cricket. We don't go to the same school, anymore. He went to Allerton Grange. I went to Roundhay. I don't do games: I am permanently exempt on medical grounds. The only time I play cricket is with Daniel. I was recently prescribed spectacles, but I don't need them to play cricket.

At the moment he goes into his run-up, Daniel is playing three roles: bowler, fielder, and umpire. Daniel is going to come steaming in from the Chelwood Avenue end, bowling towards the garage. The stumps are a big, cylindrical, metal dustbin, with a perished black rubber lid. You really need to defend your stumps in this game, if you are not going to be bowled out. If the ball hits the house, you are only out, caught if the catch is taken one-handed. If the ball goes into the gardens in the houses opposite, or gets lost under a parked car, the batting side is not allowed to run for more than four runs. The best scoring technique is to hit the ball past the bowler, so that it lands in the middle of the road, and then rolls down Chelwood Avenue, which slopes considerably. As long as the ball is visible to the fielding side, the batsmen can keep running. The current record off one ball is eleven, held by Daniel. The record score in one innings is 149, held by Daniel. Both players act as scorer. Daniel and I agree after each ball how many runs were scored, and what the total is. Sometimes we have a little talk to decide exactly what happened, but we never argue.

The bowling crease is a crack in the concrete which goes across the drive, at the top of the ramp, near the place where the drive levels out. Not only is it in the right place, but it is nice and straight, at right angles to the sides of the driveway, and has moss growing out of it, which makes it easy to see.

I get into my stance. I re-oiled my bat this morning, a yearly ritual which can only be carried out if you can find the bottle of linseed oil from last year.

Daniel delivers the ball, which is fluorescent yellow, and made by Slazenger. The ball is pitched up, and fairly quick. I play a backward defensive shot, and Daniel collects the ball. No run. I am relieved not to have lost a wicket first ball.

Brearley and Boycott meet in the middle of the wicket and have a brief talk about how the pitch is going to play.

During the first over, I realise that Daniel is bowling somewhat faster, and much more accurately than he was last summer. I also find that, as long as I manage to play the right shot, it is easier to score runs. After a while, I am going along at about 2.5 per over, which is exactly what Brearley and Boycott would do. I want to get at least to the lunch interval before Gower has to come out. Gower has been in bad form recently.

Daniel is running up again when I am distracted by movement. It is Lucian, standing in the side doorway. He is half-dressed. Daniel bowls a fast, in-swinging Yorker on the leg stump. Ding! The ball strikes the bin.

'Might that have been a bit wide?' I ask Daniel, in his

capacity as umpire. Daniel shakes his head. Brearley is on his way, and Gower will have to come out before lunch.

Lucian sits on the step in his boxer shorts and T-shirt. He has no shoes or socks on. He has a very long scab running up his left shin. He rests his arms on his knees, and regards the scene. Daniel bowls another over. Lucian sits tolerably still while I am batting. Gower and Boycott score another three runs. Derek Randall (next in the batting order) has his pads on. He is a notoriously nervous batsman.

Lucian gets up and goes back inside the house. I look at my watch and see how long it is until lunch.

I bat out another three overs without losing a wicket. Daniel seems to be using this part of the match as bowling practice. Every ball lands on the same spot at about the same speed. Once I have got used to the pace, I invent a new shot. I put my weight on my back foot, lean back, and lob the ball onto the off side, high in the air. Because it is nowhere near Daniel, he cannot catch it. Number fifteen's drive is flat, not ramped. And so Daniel has to run down his own driveway, along number fifteen's, and then back again. And because he knows where the ball is the whole time, I can run as many as I like. He tries to run me out by hurling the ball from next door's driveway, aimed at the bin, but misses by a mile. I leave the ball where it lands, on the drain filter, and I keep running. I run seven, nearly approaching Daniel's record.

My anaemic self is out of breath, but so is Daniel. Daniel stands with his hands on his hips for a while. The bowling side in this game does not have to announce itself, as the batting line-up does, but I am wondering if I have batted Daniel's Michael Holding persona out of the attack.

Lucian says, 'Can I have a bat?' Daniel and I are both

now taking on another role as stewards. Without speaking, we agree that the best way to get Lucian out of the series is to let him do what he wants to do, until he gets bored.

I offer my recently-oiled bat to Lucian, who now has a pair of slippers on. Lucian takes it.

Daniel is tossing the ball from hand to hand. Lucian gets into a stance, almost as if he is going to take this cricket seriously. The test series, for now, is on hold.

Somebody says to Lucian, 'Hang on. How many wickets do you get?' That person is me. Lucian and Daniel both look quizzical.

'Ten.'

'No you don't.'

'Why not?'

'You've only just got up,' says Daniel. Lucian is a weight-lifter, a boxer, he is four years older than us. He draws himself up and spreads his arms.

'What's that got to do with anything?'

'You get two wickets,' someone says. That person is me. Daniel nods agreement.

I lend Lucian my bat. Lucian has to be content against two fielders. I go to what would be mid-on.

Lucian takes his stance and smashes the toe of the bat repeatedly onto the drive, as if he is trying to break it. The bat does not break. Lucian looks as if he is actually waiting to receive the ball. I glance at Daniel. Daniel tosses me the ball.

I can't bowl pace, like Daniel. I bowl left-arm spin. I plant the ball in between my middle and ring fingers. I measure out my run-up. I move the piece of broken brick. I give Lucian what might be called an 'arm ball' or a 'top spinner.' I bowl it as fast as I can. He doesn't pick it. Ding! Out. Daniel holds up a finger.

'I wasn't ready,' says Lucian.

'Out,' says Daniel. 'That is the first of your two wickets.'

'But I wasn't ready.'

'You were ready, but we will bowl that ball, again.'

'I wasn't ready.'

'Whatever. We will bowl that ball, again. Play.' I go to the start of my run up. I plant the ball again between my middle and ring fingers.

This time, I give him a leg break, pitched in at an angle, about where leg stump would be. That means that the ball moves away from his legs, and he has to reach for it. He goes to hit it, reaches too far, misses it, and Ding! the ball hits the stumps.

'That wasn't really out.'

'Yes, it was,' says Daniel.

'It didn't hit anything.'

'Yes, it did. It hit the stumps.'

'No, it didn't.'

Daniel gets his own bat, and offers it to Alex, who has just re-appeared.

Lucian picks up Alex, and begins throwing him around his body.

While Lucian is throwing Alex around, Daniel and I have some Wensleydale cheese on cream crackers, with fruity sauce.

After the lunch interval, Daniel offers his bat to Lucian.

'I've got to wait until someone gets out,' Daniel says.

'I'm out,' I say. Daniel nods, indicating that by 'someone', he meant Lucian.

Lucian goes into bat, and almost immediately starts poncing around. He goes into a batting stance, and then sticks his arse out as the bowler is just about to deliver the ball. He does 'gardening' (prodding uneven parts of a grass-covered cricket pitch) on the concrete drive.

Daniel gets annoyed.

Daniel takes a slightly longer than usual run-up.

Daniel bowls a fast, middle-stump Yorker with top-spin. Lucian tries to get the bat down in time, but fails. Ding! Daniel, in his capacity as umpire, raises the finger. I do, too.

'Yeah, but you can't say that was really out.'

'Why not?'

'Well, we are just having a kick-about, aren't we? You can't really say that somebody was "out".'

'Yes, we can. If the ball hits the bin, and it's a legal delivery – which this was – you're out.'

Daniel and I both know that Lucian is probably going to get bored soon.

And then Alan arrives. Alan asks Lucian what he is doing. Lucian becomes abusive. Pauline tells both of them that she wants to walk down the street with her head held high. It occurs to me that the 'head held high' thing might work better if they discussed it indoors. Daniel and I carry on playing cricket.

Daniel starts to experiment with his bowling. He tries different angles, different points of release of the ball. He tries moving his fingers in different ways at the point of release. This variety causes me to concentrate very hard on not getting out. I take each ball as it comes. I manage to stay in for longer than I would have expected.

Daniel tries a slower ball, pitched short of a length, just outside off stump. I don't know if it is the slowness, or the way it bounces off the concrete drive, but it sits up. It is there to be hit. All I see is the biscuit-coloured pitch, the green outfield, the sun on the pavilion, and the members in their blazers and ties. I dance down the pitch to get to it, and I bring the bat through the line of the ball with strong hands. Ian Botham is momentarily promoted up the order. I whack it for six. It takes us a quarter of an hour of negotiation with the householder opposite to get the ball back. It went over his house and landed in his carp pond. Daniel tries squashing the ball to get the water out, but in his capacity as umpire, he gets another one out of the box in the garage.

I get to 180 runs. This is a new series record. It gets too dark to play. Daniel and I go upstairs to Daniel and Lucian's bedroom. Their sister, Claudine, is playing music in her bedroom. I am waiting to hear if my mother is going to ring Pauline, or if I am going to have dinner (what they call 'tea') with Daniel's family. They are deciding whether or not to have fish and chips. They are discussing the relative merits of two or three fish and chip shops.

Lucian will be going to a weightlifting competition in Bristol the following day. That means a full day's bowling at Daniel's West Indies team, at Edgbaston. I will need to be at my best to bowl to Desmond Haynes and Gordon Greenidge.

While we are waiting for Alan to come back from the fish and chip shop, Pauline tells Lucian off for practising his boxing by punching the back of the sofa. She also tells him off for picking his feet, at which point Lucian shouts at Pauline for picking on him. Daniel laughs in a corner. Claudine comes down from her bedroom, and I try unsuccessfully to catch her eye.

Daniel wins the series, hands down, but I get my feet as often as possible to the pitch of the ball, and I try new spin bowling techniques. I win the Headingley test.

Learning how to play cricket with Daniel is much better than learning it from a PE teacher, as long as you can get rid of Lucian. Lucian starts to get interested in his biological father, who lives in Germany, before the Oval. That takes him off the drive.

Their Faces Lost

Barney Walsh

So I'm on my way home from the shops – everyone masked, wearing masks over the normal masks of their faces – one fuck-awful Saturday afternoon, struggling under more bulging carrier bags than I can really cope with, rainwater dripping down the back of my neck and oozing into my shoes, when from nowhere a memory pops into my head. It brings me to a stop right there in the street, I gasp at the surprise of it. This funny little memory of being a small child, up past my bedtime and sneakily listening in on a grownups' private conversation. The weird thing, though, is that it's not one of *my* memories – nothing like it's ever happened to me, I'm totally sure of that. And yet there it is, floating before my mind's boggling eyes, this scarily clear vision of someone else's past. I stand there in the rain like an idiot, gaping at it, wondering where it can have come from. Another person's memory, a stowaway in my head.

I remember just as if it'd happened to me – though it *hadn't* – remember being very small, maybe only three or four years old, crouched unseen in the dark at the top of a flight of stairs, peering down between the bannisters at a living room below me. There, a man and a woman are talking. At least, the man's talking – the woman seems just to be listening, or not listening, in silence. She's in a green dress, sits perched on the edge of the sofa, leaning forwards, her hands clasped in her lap. Eyes fixed on the back of the man's head. He's at the window, looking out at the garden and the backs of houses beyond it, at leafless trees skeletal in dimming light. I see it all so clearly – in fact this odd little memory I've suddenly been gifted is way clearer than most of my own, real memories ever seem to be – clear enough anyway that I can see or remember seeing the man's lips moving, reflected faintly in the glass ... though not clear enough for me to tell what he's saying. Like I've got, or the memory's true owner has, a surer grasp of images than sounds. I guess that's normal. But whatever his words are, they're not meant for a child's ears – I remember keeping very still, in my secret listening place, scarcely breathing, *knowing* that they're talking about me. Deciding my fate, or lamenting it, I don't know – either way, bad things were about to happen, bad things that I wasn't old enough to understand or be told about yet. I remember listening, watching, feeling very scared – and not knowing of what.

But none of this is mine. The fear, like the whole memory, belongs to someone else. I can't imagine how it can have found its way into my head. Me of all people. It's like the memory had just been floating about there in the street, lost or abandoned, bobbing on the air like wind-blown litter, waiting for someone to find it and take it home with them. Waiting for something it could latch onto, for the right kind of mind to pass through it, gathering it up. It's not mine, but I know it's a *true* memory – you can tell, you can just *feel* it. And now somehow or other the memory does belong to me.

I remember holding onto the painted wooden bannister, gripping it tight with one tiny fist, the other clutching a stuffed toy of some kind. Hugging it close to me. I'm wearing pale-coloured pyjamas, I think, with some kind of childish lettering or cartoon character on the front. In the memory

I never look directly at these things – they're too familiar to the memory's real owner – so I can't know any more about them, because this brief patch of another's life is all I've been given. I can't even tell whether I'm a boy or a girl, in the memory. But I do remember the woman suddenly spotting me. Did I make a noise, to give myself away? A little sob, a frightened whimper? I think so. Or did she just sense me there somehow, even though I was being as quiet as I could? She twists her head up to silently stare at me – at my eyes, I imagine, catching what little light reaches them, at my chubby fingers, curled round the bannister. I can see that she's been crying – her face is streaked with spoilt makeup – but has stopped now. The man still stares out at the falling night. The woman looks at me, and raises a finger to her lips – in the darkness of the stairs, I place my own fingertip on my mouth in return, promising silence. She will let me hear the man's words, whatever they are. Let me hear his ... his what? His bad news? His confession? Accusation? I wish I could remember, wish I could know what it all meant to me – or to the memory's real owner, I mean.

But I can't stand here all day like an idiot in the rain, gawping at a stray bit of someone else's childhood. Whoever they are, the woman and the man aren't *my* parents, and I've never set foot in that house, wherever it is, ever in my life. Doesn't look like it's anywhere round here, much nicer than any of the places, care homes and foster homes, I was shuffled between when I was growing up. And it's not really my memory, so why should I care? All I'm doing is standing here getting rained on. So I set off again, pretty much piss-wet-through by now. The wind had caught my umbrella earlier, twisted it into uselessness. I plod home, other pedestrians – keeping their distance from me, as if they didn't do that *before* this fucking pandemic – scurrying faster than me, cars swishing their wipers, hooting and growling at each other. The world all made of grey. I wait at the lights and cross the road, return to my tower block, pick my way through the so-called garden's rippling puddles – it'd be mostly concrete if it weren't for the weeds. I stand dripping in the graffiti-decorated lift as it clanks its way upwards, unhook from my ears my much-reused disposable mask, stuff it in my coat pocket for next time. At my door, I set down my shopping bags to fumble with my keys and finally let myself into my little flat. But all the while I can't help the fugitive memory flitting about my skull, niggling at the edges of my brain. I peel off my coat, kick away my damp shoes and socks, dump the shopping bags on the kitchen counter. The bottles clinking together. I don't wash my hands. I put the kettle on, so there'll be tea in a minute. In the other room I switch on a bar of the ancient electric fire and sit down soggily, creakingly, in the armchair. For once I don't switch the TV on right away. The memory, of course, has come to me all of a piece – it's not like a film that plays in my head, more like an object I can turn in my mind's hands, like it's some rare antique – or else a fake, old tat, worthless junk. I remember the end of it just as well as the beginning, and all of the three or four minutes that I guess stretch between them. And sitting here in my springy old chair, I examine the memory again, as if I might find some identifying mark that'd help me return it to its rightful owner.

Abruptly the man turns from the window. His hand like a blade slices the air as he makes some point emphatic. He's in dark trousers and a pale shirt, looks like he works in an office, his tie loosened and collar open. He looks directly at the woman for the first time – perhaps he could see her before, though, reflected in the glass? His face is just ordinary, he's no one I've ever seen in my actual life. He's overdue for a shave, his shirt is tight around his gut. He falls silent at last, and seems to wait for the woman's response. For her what? Her agreement, her denial, her understanding, her forgiveness? Without more to go on, I can't tell. I need the context of the rest of a life, or a little bit more of it at least, not just this one isolated memory, no matter how important or life-changing a few minutes they are. But the woman doesn't know what to say, it looks like. She hesitates, wrings her hands in her lap. And helplessly, as if seeking guidance, her eyes flick to me in my hiding place at the top of the stairs.

I sit in my chair in front of the blank-faced telly, the rain still rattling the windows of my flat. All you can see through them is another tower block, mirroring mine, the darkened or lighted squares of dozens of other people's flats, other people's lives. Where people were stuck indoors for months, where ambulances have drawn up, time and again, to ferry folk away to their sedated, ventilated deaths. It'll be night soon. I try to think of something else, *anything* else – if only to find out if I still can. Am I going to the pub tonight, or will I stay in to get drunk alone? But the pubs are closed, I'd forgotten for a moment. You drink to forget, of course. How long's it been since I last spoke to my son? The answer's too difficult to work out. Even in this crisis he's not got in touch. I think of going to make that tea, or to fetch something stronger, but this tiny flat's kitchen seems so far away. I try to think of my own life, the one I'm actually living, but there's nothing in it I want to face right now. The supermarket, the job centre, the bookie's, sometimes the pub – for so long, that's all there's been, but now ... nothing. I try to dream up my own childhood, the *real* childhood that somehow I survived and that doesn't much resemble the other that I've been given a keyhole-peek into. It won't work, I somehow can't bring any of my own, true past to mind – various schools, my kid sister, a couple long-lost friends, grimy flats, the homeless shelter that time, shitty jobs and shittier job centres – none of it. All their faces lost. The only thing that seems now to fit in my head is this strange mislaid memory that somehow I've stumbled on.

The man's head snaps round to follow the woman's gaze, and he sees me – whoever I am – hiding at the head of the stairs. Instantly I scramble over the top few steps into the gloom of the upstairs landing, push myself to my feet, flee as fast as I can through one of the doors – my bedroom, I guess – and shove it closed behind me. Already I can hear the man's footsteps thumping up the stairs after me, taking two or three at a time. The woman's voice shouting something behind him. My bedroom's curtains are shut, the room's almost totally dark, but I know my way well enough without light. I dart forwards, feel my way to the bed, then instead of getting in I slip to the floor and crawl underneath. It's dusty, I feel the awkward plastic shapes of forgotten toys and unread books – things I never had in my real life – a heap of old comics that tumbles in a tiny invisible avalanche. The carpet scratches my elbows. My hair or something gets in my eyes – it doesn't matter, I can't see anyway. I still have my favourite toy – a teddy bear or stuffed dog, I don't know, a bunny perhaps – folded tight in my arm. In the darkness I shut my eyes and wait, but it isn't long, just a few seconds, before the bedroom door bangs open, light rushes in, and I open my eyes and start squealing as the man's strong hands reach under the bed, grab my ankles and haul me out from there.

And that's the end of the memory. It's all I've been given. Perhaps it's just what would fit in my brain – maybe there was an empty space (what did I lose, then?) of precisely the right size and shape, waiting for whatever psychic flotsam it would find. I don't know how the memory's true owner can have lost it. It doesn't seem to me a thing you'd just forget – though who the fuck knows what the mind can do. Or did she, or he, die? Is that what happens when we go, our minds just drift off on the breeze – thousands more of them this year than normal – unless they happen to get snagged in some stranger's cerebral whatever? It doesn't matter. What matters is that the memory belongs to *me*, now. I sit in my chair, clutching it to my chest like some tiny, wounded animal, like a precious jewel. It's mine now, no one else's. I turn it over and over, examining it from all angles, seeing more and more detail, more of its intricate workings.

I see not just that the woman's been crying, but how thin and tired she looks. Has she been ill? Dark lines under her eyes. I can make out, in the garden's darkening twilight beyond the window, the swaying colours of forgotten washing left out on the line, and a child's miniature slide, orange plastic, standing crookedly on the grass. In the living room, there's a painting over the fireplace, a pale watercolour, but I can't remember – can't *see* – what it's of. Blurry green fields or hills, maybe a river or road. A solitary figure walking. The fireplace itself has plastic coals, lit from beneath.

The woman is barefoot, her high-heeled shoes – green to match her dress – lie together under the glass-topped coffee table. Her hair is a bright yellow, but dark roots are growing through. The man has grey speckled at his temples. As he turns to face the woman, he doesn't look angry, or cruel, not particularly – just weary. There are two wine glasses on the table, one almost empty and one nearly full, and an ashtray with a single smouldering butt balanced on its rim. There are framed photographs scattered about – on the mantelpiece, on the cabinet in one corner – but again, the memory isn't sharp enough for me to see the faces in them. The close-ups must be stored in other memories than the one I've received – the original owner might have hundreds more of the room, but I have only this. There are a few ornaments, too, creamy vague figurines, plus a painted wooden bird of bright colours, some made-up species I guess. One large picture seems to be a school photo – someone with long blonde hair, in a blue blazer and tie. It can't be me, or I mean it can't be the child whose eyes I'm seeing this memory through – I seem too little for it, for big school. So is it then my big sister or brother? Where's she, or he, now? In the other snapshots, all I can recall are the vague blobs of people's faces – they could be anyone.

The light is dying now, here in my flat – it's twilight, just as it is in the memory, though those remembered moments seem worlds away from this present reality. Beginning the climb up the second wave. My frozen meals are thawing on the kitchen table. The kettle has boiled and gone cold again. The rain has passed by for the moment, though I can still hear the wind buffeting the tower block, pressing in on my windows. It's grown so dark I can barely see, but I won't go for the light switch, not yet. I'm afraid that the shock of brightness would disperse this stolen memory for ever. And besides, I don't want to look at my now, only at this unknown stranger's then.

The man drags me out from under the bed. He won't hurt me, he loves me. Still it's frightening. He pulls me into his arms, hugs me tight – my father, if that's who he is. He's weeping and talking to me, whispering in my ears. I can't remember his words but I know he's telling me he loves me and is asking me to forgive him, please forgive him. All I feel is scared and confused. The woman appears behind him in the rectangle of light from the landing – she leans against the wall and sinks slowly to the floor, her head in her hands. I don't know what's going on, I'm too little to understand – and this small fragment of memory doesn't stretch yet as far as any greater understanding its owner may have come to later.

But *there*, I've somehow made the memory grow a little – it's reached forwards just a few seconds more. Unless my head has totally invented this new part, which I know it hasn't – you can tell what's true. And so I think that if I can only focus on the memory's bits and pieces, resolve their blurriness into clarity, then even more can be mine. I remember the crimson of the woman's fingernail, stark against the paleness of her face as she raises it to her lips, hushing me. There's half a bluish, clouded tattoo visible on the man's forearm, sticking out from under his rolled-up shirtsleeve – it suddenly seems very important that I know what it's an image of, but my mind can't quite grasp that deep, not yet. What I do feel again growing within me is the vague and complex mess of emotions that I have about these people, whoever they are, that makes me begin to weep now, sitting here in my dark cell, years later and in a different lifetime, remembering.

I've given up reminding myself that this isn't actually *my* memory. That doesn't matter any more, if it ever did. I've claimed it as mine. Finders keepers. I hold onto it, squeeze it as tightly in my mind as I can bear, certain now I can't break it – I hug it to myself like the comfort of a favourite toy. If I focus hard enough I think I can bring out the details, the secrets. The colour and pattern of the man's tie. The design on the woman's fancy hair clip – snakes, butterflies? The sharp contours of a lost toy that I find under my hand, in the musty darkness beneath my bed … and if I can only tell what it is, if I can let myself sink deep enough into the memory, then maybe this tiny pearl of someone else's consciousness, this little bubble of someone else's past, instead of fading like all memories do, might swell out to fill my mind, expanding into past and future, growing, soon to swamp all my own memories, till my mind is filled up with someone else, and all that's the old me will be gone.

Contributors

Haleemah Alaydi is a writer, poet and PhD researcher at the University of York. She holds an MA in Writing for Performance and Publication from the University of Leeds, which she completed on a Chevening award. Her poems 'Home' and 'Three Truths about Life' were published by *The Scribe* arts magazine. Her novel, *When Olive Trees Died*, was shortlisted for the 2019 Borough Press BAME Open Submission competition. Haleemah has certifications in Spoken Word Poetry Slam and International Peace Studies.

Eva Böhme graduated with a Masters in Creative Writing. She has been shortlisted for both short story and flash fiction prizes, including the Comma Press Dinesh Allirajah Prize for Short Fiction, Ilkley Festival Short Story Prize, and Retreat West Flash Fiction competition.

Jenny Booth lives in Sheffield where she writes short fiction and poetry and works as a nurse. She has had fiction published in *Brittle Star* and *Prole* magazines.

SJ Bradley is a writer from Leeds. Her short fiction has appeared in various journals and anthologies including *New Willesden Short Stories 7*, *Queen Mobs*, *Litro Magazine*, and *Untitled Books*. Her first novel, *Brick Mother*, and her second novel, *Guest*, are both published by Dead Ink.

Sarah Brooks lives in Leeds, where she's a member of the

Leeds Writers' Circle, as well as being involved with the Northern Short Story Festival Academy. She's had stories published in magazines including *Interzone*, *Strange Horizons*, and *Strix*, and won the 2017 Bare Fiction Short Story Prize, the Walter Swan Short Story Prize 2017–18, and the Lucy Cavendish Fiction Prize 2019. She's currently working on a novel about an alternative history of the Trans-Siberian Express.

Anna Chilvers is a writer, a runner, a long-distance walker, a mother, a teacher and a reader. She has three published novels, *East Coast Road* (Bluemoose Books, 2020), *Tainted Love* (Bluemoose Books, 2016), and *Falling Through Clouds* (Bluemoose Books, 2010). She has written a collection of short stories, *Legging It* (Pennine Prospects, 2012), and has also written poetry and scripts. She is currently studying for a PhD on novel writing and walking in woodland.

Melody Clarke spends her days writing funding bids and research reports for charities. Once darkness falls, she turns her pen to poetry and short fiction. An active member of the York Stanza poetry group, she performed her first invited public reading in January 2020 and has more lined up. Her memoir piece, *Waiting for the Dark Clouds to Go*, was published in *The Guardian*, and a flash fiction, *Annunciation*, was shortlisted by *Artificium*. Her poem, 'Romancing the Stoned', was published on a model sushi in 2014.

Jean Davison was a prizewinner in the Ilkley Literature Festival Short Story Competition (2018), and in the Gold Dust Polish Competition (2019) for her novel in progress. She also writes non-fiction, and her memoir *The Dark Threads* is published by Headline Accent.

Trina Garnett was inspired to write 'Dancing on Ice' after a heated debate with colleagues about the office temperature. Trina is a former *Yorkshire Post* journalist who now works in PR and social media and has worked in a variety of hot and cold workplaces. She has had short stories published in two anthologies by Comma Press and is currently writing a Young Adult novel. Twitter: @TrinaGarnett

Andrea Hardaker is a Scottish writer living in Yorkshire. Andrea was an award-winning journalist before turning her attention to fiction. She studied an MA in Creative Writing at Leeds Trinity (2017). Since then her work has been published in various magazines and publications including *Storgy Magazine* and *Firewords Quarterly*. Her stories have also featured in various anthologies including; *Shallow Creek* (Storgy Horror writing long-list), *Journeys; A Space for Words* (Indigo Dreams publication), *Portmanteau* (Indigo Dreams), *Soundwaves* (The Federation of Writers Scotland – first prize flash fiction) and *Rebels* (The Scottish Book Trust). Since finishing the academy, Andrea has begun working on a collection of short stories on a dystopian theme.

Lizzie Hudson graduated from Goldsmiths and is studying an MA at Royal Holloway, University of London. Her work has been published by *Litro*, SPAM Press, *The Grapevine*, *Strix*, and *Porridge Magazine*, amongst others. In 2020, she was selected as a finalist for David Higham Agency's virtual open day for under-represented writers. She is currently working on non-fiction around reading and classism, mental health, and mid-noughties computer games.

Jennifer Isherwood's fiction has appeared online in *Litro*,

Disclaimer, and *Long Story, Short*, and will feature in Dead Ink's *Test Signal* anthology (summer 2021). She lives in Leeds where, among other things, she is a co-organiser of the writers' social night Fictions of Every Kind.

Dan Robinson writes short fiction. He won a Northern Writers' Award in 2018 for his in-progress novel, *The Two Ys*. As an artist and writer his work often deals with place. His writing has appeared at Grizedale Arts, Ikon Gallery, Mud Office and in Goldsmith's *Goldfish* anthology. He has a PhD in site-specific art (Leeds University, 2009) and an MA in Creative Writing (Goldsmiths, 2019). He leads photography and moving image at Open College of the Arts and lives in Yorkshire. @danrleeds

Richard Smyth is a writer and critic. His work appears regularly in *The Guardian*, *The Times Literary Supplement* and *New Statesman*, and he is the author of the non-fiction books *A Sweet, Wild Note* (Elliott & Thompson, 2017) and *An Indifference of Birds* (Uniformbooks, 2020). His novel *The Woodcock* will be published by Fairlight Books in May 2020.

William Thirsk-Gaskill was born in Leeds in 1967, and now lives in Wakefield, with his wife, Valerie. They appeared in a joint performance at Wakefield Litfest 2017, called *Welcome to The Mad*. William's adaptation of his novella, *Escape Kit*, was broadcast by BBC Radio 4 in 2019. His debut collections of poetry and short fiction are available from stairwellbooks.co.uk.

Barney Walsh's short stories appeared most recently in *Cōnfingō*, *The Fiction Desk's New Ghost Stories III*, *The Forge Literary Magazine*, *minor literature[s]*, *The Lonely Crowd*, and Pin Drop Studio and the Royal Academy's *A Short Affair*. He was part of the Dark Side of the North event at the first Northern Short Story Festival. He lives in Bolton.

————

If you want to know more about the Northern Short Story Festival, check out their website: bigbookend.co.uk/nssf

Lightning Source UK Ltd.
Milton Keynes UK
UKHW040253150421
382009UK00001B/170

9 781912 436576